Man of Power 3: Back to Business

Korben Hunter

Disclaimer

All characters, situations, events, places, activities and artefacts in this story are fictional. Romeo is a fictional character, his world is fictional, the film industry he works in is a figment of imagination, the people he interacts with are fictional. This is a story written purely for entertainment and all the elements in this are fictional, created for the purpose of making the story interesting and enjoyable. Any similarity to any person, living or dead, shall be considered a coincidence for which the author and the publisher shall not be responsible.

Smashwords License Statement

This ebook is licensed for your personal enjoyment only. This ebook may not be re-sold or given away to other people. If you would like to share this book with another person, please purchase an additional copy for each reader. If you're reading this book and did not purchase it, or it was not purchased for your use only, then please visit your favourite ebook retailer to purchase your own copy. Thank you for respecting the hard work of this author.

Adult Content Warning

Please be advised that this is a very adult story, what would be called X-rated in the US content rating system and XXX by the internet rating. There are a lot of sexual situations and graphic descriptions of sexual acts between men and women contained in this story.

This story includes a lot of sexual language including many hard core terms. This is a story written for entertainment and the situations as well as the actions performed by the characters are not real nor is it advised to follow their example in real life. The story includes many examples of polygamy, polyandry, cheating, cuckolding, pseudo-incest and some elements of BDSM. This is a story from fantasy and is not meant to be followed in real life.

Readers are advised to exercise discretion while reading the story and not get immersed in it to the point that it blurs the boundaries between real and fantasy. This is meant to be fun, read it purely for enjoyment. The description of any acts in this story is not an indication that they are endorsed by the author or the publisher.

It is not the intent of the author and publisher to insult, defame, damage, degrade or demoralise any group, sect, religion, gender or industry. This a story based on fantasy written for enjoyment.

Table of Contents

Series Info
Introduction
Chapter 1 – Vikas is Back
Chapter 2 – Rhea Tells Her Friend
Chapter 3 – Who is Vansh Chaudhary?
Chapter 4 – Vansh Meets Hina
Chapter 5 – Parineeti Confesses
Chapter 6 – Rhea is Missing Vikas
Chapter 7 – Jacqueline and Kriti Meet Vikas
Chapter 8 – Kriti is Smitten
Chapter 9 – Genelia's Gift
Chapter 10 – Meeting the HR Manager
Chapter 11 – Pujita Acts with Boldness
Chapter 12 – Family Reunion at Sonali's
Chapter 13 – Quick Kitchen Visit
Chapter 14 – Vikas Rules Family Dinner
Chapter 15 – Vikas Chilling with Family
Chapter 16 – Stolen Kisses
Chapter 17 – Shriya Joins the Gym
Chapter 18 – Shriya Thanks Vikas
Chapter 19 - Parineeti Picks Up a Piece
Chapter 20 – A Quick Tryst With Sonali
Chapter 21 – Gym Memberships
Chapter 22 – Vikas Auditions a Model
Chapter 23 – Parineeti Working Hard
Chapter 24 – Vansh is Summoned by the CEO
Chapter 25 – Vikas Visits the Travel Desk
Chapter 26 – Dropping Off Parineeti
Chapter 27 – Hina Gets Good News
Chapter 28 – Kajal and Vikas Date Thailand Style
Chapter 29 – Parineeti Thinking About Vikas
Chapter 30 – Hina Enjoys Anticipation
Chapter 31 – Vikas Meets with Shilpa
Chapter 32 – Vikas and Shilpa's Private Meeting
Chapter 33 – Raj Joins the Client Meeting
Chapter 34 – Huma Uses the Copy Machine
Chapter 35 – Shilpa Tells Raj the Plan

Chapter 36 – Hina's Hard Audition
Chapter 37 – Neetu Has Lunch with Boss
Chapter 38 – Meeting the Hotel Manager
Chapter 39 – Pooja Hegde Gets the Good News
Chapter 40 – Hina Meets Parineeti
Chapter 41 – Shilpa is Smug
Chapter 42 – Hina Meets Vikas
Chapter 43 – Hina Becomes a Model
Chapter 44 – Hina Gets a Lift
Thank you
My Other Books
In the next book

Series Info

This is the third book in the series. In the first book Vikas meets Kajal, their romance grows and they get married. Vikas also takes charge of his mother-in-law - Sonali. After his marriage with Kajal, Vikas takes her and her family on their honeymoon as a family trip.

The second book covers their journey on the honeymoon during which they travel to Indonesia, Malaysia and Thailand. They also take a cruise in those parts. On this journey, it turns out that Kajal enjoys it when Vikas claims pretty girls and tells her about it.

In the third book (this one), Vikas and the rest of the family are back in Bombay and everybody goes back to their business. The first two books are available as ebooks also on the same platforms as this book.

Introduction

You must have heard the expression "It's the journey, not the destination." Keep that in mind as you read this book. I write my stories in a constant stream with things happening and days passing. During these a lot of sex happens as well which, of course, is the whole purpose of writing erotica.

There are a lot of sub-plots that start in this book, some move ahead significantly, some only a small bit. But that's all part of the game. The characters will continue, the storylines will progress in each book and hopefully you will continue to enjoy each book with these sub-plots moving forward. I am just telling you this now so you don't feel disappointed that everything that gets started in this book does not get finished.

If I wait to finish the whole story or even a big part of it, there will be a bigger gap between books and my fans (well, Vikas' fans really) don't want to wait for months for the next part. So, I hope you enjoy this book in what it brings to you and trust me to bring the next part out soon.

Chapter 1 – Vikas is Back

"Good morning, Sir." Parineeti stepped into his office with a cheerful smile.

She stood there a minute to let Vikas see her in her new outfit. She was wearing a tight fitting tank top with a floral print, and a matching miniskirt which was not reaching past her mid-thighs. She had high heels on which Vikas could see as she walked around his desk to approach his chair.

It was not evident in her demeanour but Parineeti's heart was beating very fast. She had not seen her boss for about 5 weeks and she didn't know what had changed in the meantime. Before he went on his honeymoon, he and Parineeti had become close enough that they could kiss now and then. But that was before he went on his honeymoon and mostly before his wedding.

The car ride from the wedding venue was a fond memory for Parineeti. She was riding with Vikas and he had called her his second wife in his new wife's presence. Parineeti recalled that moment regularly, especially late at night in her bedroom. The fact was though, that she and Vikas had not had a single kiss after he was married.

Parineeti really wanted to resume their previous relationship. Even after his marriage, she still held her desire to be his personal, not just his personal secretary, but his personal in every way. This morning she had changed 7 times trying to find the perfect outfit for her first post-honeymoon meeting with him. She didn't want to dress slutty, but she knew how visual men are and how often subtlety is lost on them.

After several attempts she had finally chosen the tank top and miniskirt. This skirt showed her long, shapely legs but wasn't totally slutty. Her big boobs were well supported by the top and there was a small amount of cleavage, just enough to draw the eye but not so deep she would look like the heroine of a c-grade movie.

On her approach she was very clear. She had to be bold and behave like she did before his marriage. She had sat on his lap a few times and she had started to establish a routine of kissing him when saying goodnight. She had not had much time to fully establish that routine before his wedding because they were both so busy. Now, she wanted to continue all that and make it so a good morning kiss and goodnight kiss were part of their daily routine. She was sure she could build it from there.

Still, approaching him now, the last two feet before getting right next to him, Parineeti could feel her legs shaking a bit. In her head, she had already practiced this many times, how she would walk up to him, turn to left, lower her butt on his lap, put her arm around his shoulders…

Also, in her head, she had imagined this going various ways. From the best scenario where she ended up bent over his desk to the worst where he chided her and told her he could not keep her on as his secretary under the circumstances. Last night she had dreamt that he had given her a contract to sign whereby she became fully his property.

The mental practice came in handy and Parineeti smoothly lowered her butt to her boss' lap and put her right arm around his shoulders.

"Hello Sir." She smiled at him, her heart still stuck in her throat.

"Hello darling." Vikas closed his arms around her slender body and pulled her close.

Now, Parineeti lost her nervousness. She leaned in and kissed Vikas on the lips. It was a slow, casual kiss with lips open and tongues touching but not going into hot, heavy make out territory.

"Hmmm, you are becoming a better kisser." Parineeti smiled as they parted "Your wife's been teaching you?"

"Something like that!" Vikas grinned.

It was deliberate that Parineeti had mentioned his wife casually. She wanted to hint that she was happy to be on his lap and kiss him while knowing well that he was married.

"How was your honeymoon?" She asked while staying on his lap.

"It was good. How was your holiday?" Vikas kept his arm around her and caressed her back.

"Very nice. Thank you. Jackie said she will thank you herself personally." Parineeti grinned "You know what that means!"

"I do indeed." Vikas remembered how slutty Jacqueline was and how she expressed gratitude with a full-on make-out kiss.

"You asked me to bring bikini pics of me." Parineeti said tongue-in-cheek "Do you want me to email them to you or show you now?"

"Well, we have a lot of catching up to do. Let's go out for lunch and have a proper catch up." Vikas said.

"Sure, Sir." Parineeti could hardly contain her excitement "I will make the reservation. SpiceKlub?"

"Yes, that's fine."

Chapter 2 – Rhea Tells Her Friend

"Sonal! You bitch! Give me my phone back." Rhea screamed chasing her friend around the desks.

"I will." Sonal said, climbing on a desk and staying out of Rhea's reach "I just want to see your wallpaper."

Before Rhea could reach her Sonal turned on Rhea's phone screen and looked at her lock screen wallpaper.

"Oh!" Sonal said in a perplexed voice "Who is that? I thought you had your new filmstar crush on it."

Rhea didn't reply and Sonal gave the phone back.

"Who is that?" Sonal persisted "Is it a hero from the South Indian films?"

"No!" Rhea had to answer "It's my jiju."

"He's very handsome." Sonal said "I saw him at the wedding, but he looks different in casual clothes, very sexy though."

"Isn't he?" Rhea agreed "He's like a filmstar himself."

"Where is the photo from? Looks like a beach."

"Yes, it was on his honeymoon. You do remember I was gone for a month?"

"Of course." Sonal said "But I didn't know you were going with him on his honeymoon.

"I did. We all did. He took the whole family."

"Wow! That's amazing. Where did you go?"

And for the next one hour Rhea told Sonal all about her trip and how wonderful her brother-in-law was.

"You love him, don't you?" Sonal said.

Rhea paused at being caught like that but then nodded "I am pathetic, aren't I?"

"Can't say that." Sonal said "He is awfully handsome. And from what you have told me he's very sweet as well. He is very rich and powerful but he takes care of the whole family."

"Exactly! You do get him. He's so wonderful."

"Yeah, not many men like that around." Sonal said "Usually men get a little power, they become dictators."

"Not jiju, he's not a dictator." Rhea said "More like a benevolent king."

"Dude, you are totally in love with him." Sonal said.

"I know." Rhea sighed "But can you blame me?"

"No, can't blame you really." Sonal agreed "If I met someone like that I would go crazy for him to0."

"Even if he were married?"

"Well, he's only married to your sister." Sonal pointed out "Saali aadhi ghawali, no?"

"That's what I keep telling him!" Rhea said excitedly.

"What does he say?"

"Nothing. He just keeps being himself, charming, sweet, sexy, but completely appropriate."

"That's a shame when you clearly want him to do you."

Rhea turned her phone screen on and held it in front of Sonal.

"Ok, ok," Sonal said "I get your point. Now turn that off. It does something to me. Actually, send a copy of that photo to me."

"Why? Are you sweet on him suddenly?"

"It's not like I want to push him down on that wet sand and ride him like a stallion," Sonal said "but he is easy on the eyes."

"Sonal, what will I do?" Rhea moaned.

"Nothing!" Sonal said firmly "He's your brother-in-law. Your sister's husband!"

"What would you do if he was your brother-in-law?"

"I would climb in his bed one night and pretend like I am my sister."

"My sister sleeps with him, you know?" Rhea reminded her.

"Not in my head." Sonal shook her head "In my head, he sleeps alone and completely nude."

"You little slut!" Rhea elbowed her "You are totally picturing jiju naked."

"Will you introduce me some time?"

"Sure. But then don't blame me if you fall in love with him, too."

"I don't fall in love, baby, I fall in lust." Sonal said "That's more my style."

"Yeah, I know. Did you fuck that one, what was his name, Nakul?"

"Haha, yes, but I have had two more since Nakul." Sonal said proudly.

"You little tramp!"

"Well, you were gone for a whole month." Sonal protested "I had no entertainment. It's not I had a hunk of a brother-in-law to snuggle with."

"Oh, Sonal, I forgot to tell you," Rhea said excitedly "One night, I did get in the bed with him."

"Really? Wow."

"Yes, this was on the ship. Kajal and Jiju were watching a movie, and I just…"

Chapter 3 – Who is Vansh Chaudhary?

Vansh was not a big fan of irony but even he could not deny that his life was full of it. He had always been a shy kid who had grown up into a shy adult. This shyness of his had always directed him towards things that could be done alone or indoors, or both.

His parents had got him a small camera for his 12th birthday. It had very quickly become his obsession. He spent so much time with it that it was inevitable that he would become good with it. His parents were very proud of it and their house was full of photographs that he had taken.

The irony was that the parents who were very proud of his photography skills and could not stop talking about it to relatives, had been horrified when he had expressed an interest in joining an art school to become a photographer. What, he would become one of those people who carried around a camera bag in a wedding and took pictures of people while they were trying to eat in peace? What would people say? And those people were always starving. None of them ever seemed to make any real money. It was such an uncertain field. No, no, Vansh must do something more practical and useful that would get him a job and a career – like software engineering. If he wanted to carry on taking photos on weekends for his own pleasure, why, there was no harm in that. No harm at all.

Computers like the camera was another thing that could be done indoors and mostly alone or with other humans far away by means of the internet. Vansh had excelled at it. He had passed the graduate degree with distinction and then postgraduate degree with first class.

Another irony in his life was that even in the early stages of photography when he realised that he might be able to get some real skill with camera, he wanted to become a fashion photographer. The allure was, of course, the pretty girls that he would get to photograph and, hopefully, date. But he was still pathologically shy and while he was great behind the camera, just holding the camera did not give him the courage to talk to them.

Vansh had left Pune in the hope that he would be able to find a better job in Bombay. The truth was that he wanted to live alone and have a social life which he could not do in Pune where he had to live with his parents. So, after doing a few small IT jobs in Pune for a couple of years, he had gathered enough courage to lie to his parents that he had received an offer for a good job from a company in Bombay. They had been a little sad but Pune and Bombay are hardly 3 hours drive away and they had accepted the fact that their little bird had grown up and wanted to fly. Vansh had moved to Bombay.

In Bombay, he had struggled for a while, holding on to the hope of becoming a professional photographer. He visited many studios and newspaper offices to see if anybody would hire him. While having a degree in photography is by no means a requirement in the photography profession, it can help one to produce some kind of background which gives the potential employer some confidence into the candidate. Vansh had no background and simply producing example of his work somehow didn't seem to get him the jobs he wanted. He did get some offers for freelance work and he gave it a shot but the work was not well-paid or regular. He was eating into his savings and feeding his camera the same thing. But it could not go on forever.

After he missed the rent payment twice in a row and the landlord gave him a printed eviction notice, Vansh had to accept that he will need to find a job in the field where he had the qualification if for no other reason than to keep body and soul together. He still wanted to live in Bombay and for that he would need money. Somehow the hopeful air of the city had infected his spirit and he felt like some day he would be able to realise his dreams if he just stayed in Bombay.

The job that Vansh found was another great, and cruel, irony in his life. He found a job in an ad agency. It was a medium sized ad agency and Vansh would have given his first-born to get a chance there. In fact, he had tried it in within the first week after he moved to Bombay, but was told that without relevant qualifications they would not even consider his application.

But, the second time, when he came around, desperate for money to survive, they had been happy to accept his application and make him an offer on the same day. Because he had applied in the IT department this time. So, Vansh was working in his dream company just two floors down from his dream job, stuck in a job that he could do really well but hated with his guts. Even in a life so stacked with irony, this was not the supreme irony of his life. That honour was reserved for his girlfriend.

Everybody knew, including Vansh, that Hina was way too hot for him. By rights, she was way out of league. Yet, she was his girlfriend, because of the simple fact that he was a photographer even though he wasn't. He had come across her in the last stages of his struggle. She had been rejected as a model from the same modelling agency where Vansh had been rejected as a photographer. They had literally collided on their way out and bonded over their similar misfortune.

Hina had been struggling in Bombay as a model for more than twice the length that Vansh had been trying to get a job as a photographer. As a model you didn't need qualifications but you did need a shitload of luck. Hina was gorgeous but also smart. She had found a job as a waitress in the very first month that she had landed in Bombay from her small village via Delhi. It had taken her a long time to make this journey from J&K to Bombay for reasons similar to Vansh's own story.

She was determined to make it big in show business but each year as her age rose, her hopes became a little more unrealistic and her struggle became a little more desperate. She had come to Bombay when she was just about to become 30 and while she didn't look more than 22, she was competing against real 22 year olds who looked 18. Now after a couple of years while she still looked stunning, her competition was getting more fierce not less. But she was a realist. She worked her waitress job to pay for her food and rent, and took advantage of the shift timings to continue her struggle. Now it had just become habit. She took rejections in her stride and still continued to register with any talent agency she found promising and paid the registration fee willingly.

It's not that Hina didn't know how the industry worked or that she was unwilling to pay the price for fame and fortune. She knew that even to get a good portfolio made a girl had to sleep with the photographer. To get an actual modelling gig, a girl had to sleep with…well, whoever was calling the shots. But she was not prepared to sleep with just anyone. If it were a photographer, it would have to be a good photographer, if it were a producer or agency head, she better have a chance at getting the job before she would spread her legs for them.

The problem with this thinking is that there are more of the models and fewer of the photographers and talent agents. This dynamic is so skewed in their favour that even a crappy photographer with a half-room studio that he sleeps in at night can "date" two or three different girls a week. For bigger ones where Hina aimed, she could not even get her foot in the door. She had assessed this situation quickly and managed to get her portfolio made by a photographer who was not completely crap. She had slept with him twice, showered like crazy after each time, and then never headed that way again.

Sadly, that portfolio which cost her money every time she got copies made, had been tossed into too many wastebaskets around the town. It was after another such wasted and soul-breaking afternoon that Hina had met Vansh while coming out of the agency after hearing "Sorry, we are not looking for amateurs at this time. Leave your headshot, we'll call you."

Chapter 4 – Vansh Meets Hina

Vansh and Hina had gotten along fine right from start. They had gone out to various tourist spots and even for dinner when they could afford to eat out. Vansh was very attracted to her simply because…well, she was stunning. Her non-existent career notwithstanding, she was model material from head to toe. She had a great fashion sense and dressed bold in a way that looked hot and adorable at the same time. Why she hung out with him, Vansh never new. The few friends that he had now were also never sure why she was with him.

But she was with him. There was no doubt about that. Vansh would probably never have got the courage but it was Hina who had initiated their first kiss. It was on a rainy afternoon, when they were waiting out the rain under a shop awning that she had simply leaned in and kissed him. On the lips. Just like they do in the movies. It would have grown into something more but Vansh was never comfortable with such behaviour in public. It had taken him a long time to hold her hand when they were out. Hina had a shift right after that and after she had gone, Vansh had walked home in the rain, happy as the cat who has licked the cream off the milk and gotten away unwatched.

That weekend, when Hina and Vansh both didn't have a job to go to, they had had sex. He had loved it. She was his first and Vansh had loved every moment of it. Hina had told him it was great. They had done more of that. And many more times since then. Given Hina's schedule and her dedication to doing the rounds of studios and agencies in her spare time, they didn't have sex very often, but he liked knowing that they could, any time. They were a couple.

He loved her and he was sure that she loved him too. They had not really talked about it, but he knew that he wanted to spend his life with her. They had celebrated their first anniversary a couple of months ago, and his friends had openly said that they were jealous of him. Yes, the same bastards who used to tease him that he was dating above his level, were now jealous of him. He loved that.

A big problem that he could foresee in his otherwise wonderful future was his parents. He had not yet told them about Hina. He wasn't sure how they would react to him wanting to marry a Muslim girl. They were quite progressive normally, but people behave weirdly when it's a question of religion or their children's marriage, and this was both. Still, having been with her for more than a year, he was thinking about taking a chance and doing it now. He had a plan to take her home with him on Diwali and introduce her to his family.

It would help if Hina got a modelling break before then, everybody knew, the normal rules didn't apply to show business people. Or if by some miracle, he himself managed to get his photography career started, it would be the same thing. But Vansh knew that those two things were very uncertain and improbable while the date for Diwali was already fixed. It would be here in a couple of months. It was weird that the two uncertain things actually happened but the certain thing didn't happen. Diwali never came for Vansh that year.

Not only did Hina get a great break in modelling, Vansh himself got an amazing job as a photographer, but sadly, he lost Hina in the process. And that, was the supreme irony of his life.

Here's how it happened. On Hina's last birthday, they had gone out to the zoo and as usual Vansh had taken his camera with him. Somehow the conversation had turned towards their careers and Hina had mentioned that it was weird that she was dating a photographer and yet, he had never done a photoshoot of her.

"What are you talking about?" He said "I take photos of you all the time."

"I am not talking about snaps." Hina said "I mean a photoshoot, like a proper photoshoot for a portfolio. Headshots and such."

"Babe, I don't have a studio, you know that."

"You don't need a studio." Hina said "We can do an outdoor shoot. The city is full of interesting backdrops."

That made Vansh think. They talked about it and even scouted the city for good backdrops for portrait photos. Then a week after their anniversary they finally did it. They got photos done in various different places and did a final part of the shoot in Hina's apartment. Vansh edited them and the output was like a professional portfolio. Hina was really happy with it. She started using that instead of her two-year old crappy portfolio.

It was a good enough set of photos that Vansh could use it as his portfolio as well. He had still not lost hope that some day he would be a photographer in this same company. The photography department was just two floors above the IT floor. But to Vansh, that was a 100-mile journey. The agency made many video ads and print ads. For video ads the crews were usually hired from outside, but for print ads they had a couple of photographers in-house who did the job. Vansh knew he had no hope of being considered if he applied again.

His only chance was to talk directly to the CEO, show him his work and somehow persuade him to try him out. He had never met the CEO but he had seen him in company events and he was a young guy, well, not as young as Vansh, but definitely not CEO-age. Vansh argued that he would be open to new ideas and taking chances on people. But taking a bold action like that was not in Vansh's character.

"Baby, you have to take the chance." Hina said when he told her his idea.

"It's just that he's very busy, and I don't want to…I mean I will look like a fool if he…"

"Ok, ok." Hina knew about Vansh's shy and oftentimes timid character and while she didn't like it, she always made allowances for it "How about you send him an email, attach the best photos to that email and write a cover letter explaining who you are and what you want?"

Anything that could get him out of an uncomfortable social situation was always welcome in Vansh's world. He liked the email idea.

It proved harder than he had thought. He created the email, attached the photos, wrote a cover letter, but he could not click Send. He had a grave feeling that he was making a fool of himself. He was not a photographer. He was the IT guy. Why would the high-ranking CEO who ran this big company, waste time on his dreams and aspirations? He could see it in his mind's eye that the CEO will get the email, make a face and delete it. Vansh left the email in the Drafts folder.

For a few days, Hina asked him if he had sent the email. Vansh had made some excuse. She tried reminding him that it could be good for her career as well as his.

"Baby, VisCom does so many projects, they are growing like a rocket." She said "They must need a lot of models. I have already applied there but always been told that they don't hire directly. Can you imagine if my photo caught the CEO's eye? It could be the making of my career."

"Yes, yes, of course." Vansh agreed.

"Just a couple of projects from VisCom," She persisted "even print ads, could get me started. God knows, I am not getting anything anywhere else, and I don't want to be a waitress all my life. I want to do some modelling while I am still young and pretty."

Vansh agreed "You are right. I will send it on Monday."

But that Monday never came. He always lost his nerve at the last moment. The email lived in his Drafts folder for over a month. Then the CEO got married and went on a month-long holiday for his honeymoon. Vansh cursed himself.

Last night after a wonderful weekend, Vansh and Hina had a bad fight that somehow turned towards his unwillingness to send the email to the CEO. In her anger, Hina even accused him of being petty and jealous. She said he didn't want her to be successful because he was intimidated by her.

As he walked to work this morning from the station, the fight was still fresh in Vansh's mind and he was wondering if there was any truth in what Hina said. He knew that the CEO was joining back from today. The email was still lying in Vansh's Drafts folder. He looked at the large words "Visual Communications" as he entered the door under them and crossed the lobby of the big building.

He took the lift to his floor, walked to his office and sat down. His colleagues had not arrived yet. Vansh always arrived half an hour before starting time. He sat down, turned on his computer and pulled out the single email from the Drafts folder. He read the message again for the thousandth time:

"Dear Mr. Malhotra,

Please allow me to introduce myself. I am Vansh Chaudhary, I work in the IT department of VisCom…."

The nerves were still there. His hand was shaking a little. But today, he was angry. How could Hina said that he didn't want her to succeed? There was some guilt mixed with the anger, was she right, was he insecure? And there was a little hope too, what if the boss didn't delete the email, what if the face he made was a thoughtful, critical face, what if he replied….

Vansh steadied his hand and typed the email address in the "To:" field "Vikas Malhotra". He pressed Control-K. The name became underlined. The address was correct. Only one thing left to do…one little thing…

He clicked Send.

"Phew!" He expelled his breath noisily.

Chapter 5 – Parineeti Confesses

SpiceKlub was not the most posh restaurant in Bombay but it was close. Their trade was usually CEOs, top management and celebrities. This was quite in contrast with the Indian street food which was their speciality but that's how Bombay is – a study in contradictions.

Vikas and Parineeti were welcomed by the head waiter as they entered. They were regulars there and the staff knew them. They were shown to their private booth without any wait. Vikas usually preferred the booth away from the crowd instead of taking a table by the window. For business lunches it provided fewer distractions to be away from the window as well as the crowd.

"So, now tell me what fun did you have in Goa?" Vikas asked Parineeti once they settled in their booth, sitting side by side.

"Goa was amazing, Sir." Pari took out her phone and showed him some photos.

"The bikini photos as per your orders." She said.

"Beautiful!" Vikas took the phone and swiped through the photos slowly "You look even hotter than I thought."

"You are so sweet, Sir." Parineeti kissed his cheek. She was sitting very close to him, peering over his shoulder, even though she didn't need to see the pictures.

"Very nice. And did you go ahead from there to other places as you had planned?"

"Yes, Sir. We went to Rajasthan and Agra, you know, just for the Taj." Parineeti replied "And by the way, I really, really want to go to the Taj Mahal with you some time. I missed you so much there."

He put his arm around her and squeezed her softly "Of course, darling. Why not?"

They had a leisurely lunch and talked about their respective holidays. Parineeti fussed over him and served him during lunch, she listened to his stories and asked questions. She stayed very close to him, staying in his intimate space most of the time.

"By the way, did you like my outfit? I bought this in Goa." She said leaning back so he could see her skimpy top and short skirt again.

"Of course, it looks great, I said so this morning - you look sensational." Vikas smiled.

"Thank you, Sir. And if HR calls me in, you'll have to save me. I am worried they will haul me in that my skirt is too short or something."

"Well, they don't need to bother with that. Your skirt is none of their business. After all, you are my personal, right?"

A wide smile lit up Parineeti's face "Yes, Sir. You remembered!"

She was referring to the drunk phone call she had made from Goa to Vikas when he was on the cruise.

They stayed for dessert after the main meal. Vikas ordered ice cream while Parineeti ordered an Indian dessert called "Ras Malai".

"Would you like a taste, Sir?" Parineeti offered.

"Sure. Thanks."

Instead of pushing the plate towards him, Parineeti took a little spoonful and fed him with her own hand. He took it.

"Very nice."

"Ah, you eat like a child." Parineeti said which was an unfair comment on Vikas' eating habits but it did give Parineeti the excuse to wipe the little drop of sugar syrup from the corner of his lips.

"Thank you, darling."

Parineeti leaned in and kissed him. Her hand was placed gently at the back of his neck. She pulled him closer and pressed her lips on his. Vikas kissed her back, slowly sucking her bottom lip into his mouth. The slow kiss was very intimate and they both took their time with it. Vikas' tongue parted her lips and Parineeti sucked it into her mouth. Their lips pressed harder against each other as the hot and wet kiss continued. Their breaths mingled in an erotic blend and their bodies pressed in a tight hug.

"Mmmm, that was a better dessert." Vikas commented with a smile.

Parineeti looked into his eyes and said "Can I ask you something, Sir?"

"Sure, babe."

With a little hesitation, she started "Ummm, Sir, it's normal, like with Jackie's boss, too, and other companies, I mean our company, too, you know, normally bosses, and their personal secretaries, like, I am sure you know…." She took a breath and looked up in his eyes again "How come you never took possession of me, Sir?"

Vikas smiled cupped her cheek in his hand and replied slowly in a gentle tone "I didn't want to ruin your life, honey. You were a young girl under my protection. A young, beautiful girl," he added "working under me, in my protection. You have a boyfriend and I saw no reason to ruin your life just for my enjoyment, or to satisfy my primal urges."

"I had a boyfriend, Sir. I don't any more. Haven't had one for months. And it would not have mattered. I would have left him if you wanted, or kept him on the side, or whatever you said. I would have loved to belong to you." Summoning her courage she added "I would love to belong to you."

Keeping his arm around her slim waist, Vikas pulled her close "You are forgetting that I am married, darling."

"I am not talking about marriage, Sir, just that it would be nice to be yours."

"Okay, I won't bullshit you. There were these superhot waitresses on the cruise we took. Like, I am talking supermodel hot, and in fact, most of them were failed models. There were 4 of them in First Class on the cruise. I did nail all of them. So the marriage excuse is not 100% valid. But they were models, they knew what they were doing and having sex with me won't affect their life in any profound way."

Vikas took a breath and continued in a slow, patient tone "But you, you are special. I can't treat you as casually, and on the other hand you can't have a future with me. I am indeed married and you are still a beautiful, young girl under my protection. Some day soon you will find someone worthy of you and you will live happily ever after. I don't want to be the one mistake in your past that you look back at and regret."

"You are not a mistake, Sir." Parineeti tried to argue "But I…"

"No, sweetheart. I cannot help myself to you just because you are a sweet girl and somehow under the impression that you like me."

"I don't like you, Sir." Parineeti said firmly "I love you!"

"That too." Vikas said and pulled her in for a tight hug signalling the end of discussion.

Parineeti shut up and tried to keep her moist eyes from dripping as she clung to him tightly.

Chapter 6 – Rhea is Missing Vikas

"I miss Jiju!" Rhea wailed "It was so nice on the cruise. Why did we have to come back?"

She was looking at the photos from the trip on her tablet.

"We had to come back some time, baby!" Sonali said, looking over her shoulder.

"Doesn't Jiju look so handsome in this tropical shirt?" Rhea said.

"Well, he's a handsome boy. He looks good in suits and also in tropical shirts." Sonali said casually "And he's kind which is even more important."

"Mumma, in the old days kings used to have many queens, no?" Rhea said.

"Yes, they did. So?"

"Well, Jiju is like a king, he's very powerful and strong."

"What are you trying to say, Rhea?" Sonali asked even though she knew that Rhea was smitten with her brother-in-law.

"Nothing mumma. Just saying Jiju is like a king and he looks great in photos."

"Yes, he does. We should get some prints made from these pictures to put in frames in the house. Will you select some, please?"

"Oh wow, great idea, mumma."

"And don't select only pictures of your jiju, huh?" Sonali reminded her "I would like some pictures of the rest of the family as well."

"Of course, I won't select just jiju's pictures." Rhea said although that's what she had been thinking about doing.

Chapter 7 – Jacqueline and Kriti Meet Vikas

"Hello Sir." Jacqueline chirped as she entered Vikas' cabin.

Vikas looked up "Hi, Jackie."

Jacqueline completely ignored Kriti Sanon who was following her and went around Vikas' desk to hug him. He got up and accepted her in his arms. Her hug was already too tight and inappropriate for office but then she leaned in and pressed her lips on his. To Kriti's surprise the boss didn't pull back but kissed her back. From the way their heads moved, Kriti could easily see that Jacqueline's lips were open and she was sucking Vikas' tongue in her mouth. His hands were rubbing her back up and down, including the top part where his fingers were playing on her bare back.

Kriti had noticed and wondered at Jacqueline's tight, deep neck tube dress in the morning, but now she saw the reason. Jacqueline was rubbing her bare thighs on his legs as they hugged and kissed so tightly. Kriti wondered if he would expect her to do the same. She was not sure she could do that with someone she was just meeting for the first time. But Kriti had other girlfriends who worked similar jobs and she knew that all of them submitted to their bosses as a matter of course. Most of the times the bosses were married but it didn't stop them from fucking the girls in their office or in a hotel room as they got the opportunity. One of the girls was even married but her boss still fucked her regularly. Her husband also knew about it and more than once the boss had fucked her at her own home.

After Jacqueline's warning in the morning, Kriti had gone out and bought a nice outfit. It consisted of a nice white top and an asymmetrical miniskirt. The top was white silk and deeply sleeveless. The back was mostly bare. It had a deep cut with frills around the V-neck. It was only long enough to go 2 inches below her breasts which left her flat belly bare including her navel. The top was thin and fitted, leaving no space for a bra, especially with the bare back but it supported her firm, shapely tits without crushing them.

The skirt was low-rise and started on her hips, covering her ass crack in a way that made Kriti aware to not bend over. The fabric was a mix of cotton and synthetic. There was only one waistband but below that the skirt was in two layers, both see-through to a different degree. The inner layer of the skirt was like a micro mini, covering her pussy and ass but just barely. The outer layer was a few inches long in an asymmetrical style. On her right leg it started on her mid-thigh, on the left leg it covered her mid-thigh. The outer layer was see-through enough that her fair thighs showed through when she stood or walked, but if she stood against a strong light, even the inner layer would be fully see-through and anyone would get a good view of her ass and her white lace thong.

Kriti felt that it was too sexy for office, but it was the one outfit that she liked and she didn't want to waste her money on something she would not wear after today. Even then it had blown her fashion budget for the whole month and she had no money left to buy shoes. For today, she would just have to survive in her business shoes, tomorrow she could wear a pair of high heels from home. She had loads of them.

When she got back to office, Jacqueline had complimented her outfit "Now you look something I can present to boss."

She had lent Kriti a pair of black 7" high heels for the day. Her final advice to Kriti was to get rid of her panties.

"But - " Kriti had started and Jacqueline had raised her hands "I am just giving advice, follow, don't follow up to you."

Kriti had sighed and removed her panties. She had put them in her bag.

Now she wondered if that fact would become pertinent in this meeting. It was obvious that he had already fucked Jacqueline and Kriti was sure that if he wanted her, she would not have a choice to say no. Still, he was a good looking man. She had seen the photos of two of her friends' bosses and they were pot-bellied, middle-aged man who would tip the scale towards unattractive. The others, she had heard were no better looking. On the contrary, Vikas Malhotra was a handsome man, handsome enough that Kriti would be happy to date him if he were not married. Actually, even now…no, no, she could not have an affair with a married man. But then, if he was her boss and he wanted her under him, she would not have an option but to surrender. Yes, that was it, she would have to surrender to his power, not because she wanted to but she had no choice.

All that went through Kriti's head while Jacqueline greeted her boss with more intimacy than some girls had with their boyfriends. Then finally, she stepped back and half-turned towards Kriti.

"Sir, this is my colleague Kriti Sanon, she joined while I was gone. She will be working under me as junior exec for PR." Jacqueline pointed to Kriti "Kriti, Vikas Sir, our CEO."

Kriti took a quick breath and got ready for his next demand. Would he pull her in for a hug or kiss her like he had just kissed Jacqueline. Well, her outfit was quite skimpy he would be able to grope her well. Kriti got ready.

"Welcome to the team, Kriti. Looking forward to working with you." Vikas said "Come, shall we sit there?" He gestured towards the conference area in his office.

It would be unfair to say that Kriti was looking forward to having Vikas grope her in the first greeting but she did feel a bit let down as he didn't even shake hands with her. Was she not pretty enough? Was her outfit too slutty? Or not slutty enough? Alright, yes, she was looking forward to same kind of hug as Jacqueline even though it was totally unreasonable considering she had just met him.

"Beautiful outfit, Kriti." Vikas said as they moved towards the sofas "You look great."

"Thank you, Sir." Kriti's heart jumped in her chest. Okay, he had noticed her. He thought she was pretty. Kriti couldn't understand why it mattered but his approval had suddenly made her feel so much lighter and happier.

Vikas sat on one of the long sofas and Jacqueline promptly sat next to him on the same sofa. Kriti had to settle for the sofa chair at right angles with this sofa. She was on Jacqueline's side, so while Jacqueline was sitting so close that she was practically in his lap, Kriti was nowhere close. Again, she didn't understand why it mattered but she wanted to sit close where he could touch her like he was keeping Jacqueline close with his arm around her waist. He was keeping them both in the conversation but Kriti was only getting his eye contact whereas she could see his hand rubbing lightly on Jacqueline's back. Kriti thought about sitting next to him on the other side of him, but that would be awkward and she could lose the eye-contact as well.

"Sir, can I interrupt a minute?"

Kriti knew the girl peeking in the door was Vikas' personal secretary Parineeti Chopra. She deserved to be his personal, she was gorgeous.

"Yes, come in, darling." Vikas said.

Parineeti came in and easily sat on her knees beside him on the floor. She opened a file and placed it on his lap. She stayed close and wrapped her arm around his thigh, pressing her body close to his leg from the side.

"This is the list of the crew they have sent over from CP, Sir." Parineeti said "They have said, they can give you a more detailed presentation whenever you want."

"Hmmm, who is the head of Videography, have them look at it?"

"We don't have any, Sir." Parineeti said "We are looking for one, but we haven't recruited one yet."

"Okay, I will talk to Rani about that. Who is looking at this now?"

"Rishi Sir and Shweta look at these things sometimes." Parineeti was staying close to him as they discussed things. She was completely in his personal intimate space and Kriti could see his left hand resting on her back while she held the file open.

"Hmm, alright, ask Shweta to look at these things specifically," He looked for a pen and Parineeti put one in his hand, he underlined a few items "and tell me what questions to ask. Then call Shilpa and arrange for the presentation."

"Yes, Sir." Parineeti took the file and went away. They continued with their meeting.

Kriti noticed that Jacqueline was sitting with one leg placed flat on the sofa. She could see that Vikas would be getting a direct look at her pussy from his angle. Of course, Jacqueline was not wearing any panties. She had got Kriti to remove her panties before bringing her to the boss, how could she herself wear panties? Kriti also uncrossed her legs and turned a little more towards Vikas. If he noticed her bare pussy under her short skirt, he didn't give any indication of it. He continued to include them both in the discussion. Kriti was feeling very anxious that she was missing her chance. This was her first impression on him and she wanted him to not only notice her but feel that she was a good girl who would cooperate whenever he decided to take her under his control.

She had already forgotten her previous logic that she was only going to surrender to him if he made her. She was a good girl, not some slut who would lust after her handsome boss even when she knew he was married. But Kriti was feeling a deep craving inside her to make sure that he noticed her, not just as an employee but as a pretty girl. A pretty girl who was available. Again, this thought surprised her. She was never an easy girl. The boys she dated called her a shy girl. The less nice ones called her a cocktease. But both types knew that it was not easy to get her in bed. Then why was she suddenly throwing herself at a man who was older, married and her boss? Kriti didn't know. But the thought of leaving his office without making some sort of progress was making her very anxious. She was jealous of how close and intimate Jacqueline was with him. She was no longer thinking of her as inappropriate, she was thinking of her as lucky. Then Kriti got her chance.

"Yes, Sir." Jacqueline said "Kriti has done a couple of case studies about that. There are two approaches we can take based on who we partner with. Kriti can explain better, she has made some slides."

Kriti had brought her office tablet with her. Her Powerpoint presentation was on it. She picked up the tablet and quickly moved to kneel on the rug in front of him. Instead of sitting next to him to show him the presentation which would have been normal, Kriti boldly moved to the rug in front of him and sat on her knees in the exact position she would have taken if he had asked her to suck his dick. She knew that and she wanted him to think about that as well.

Sitting up on her knees, she placed the tablet on his thighs, facing him. She showed him the presentation, talking about the slides but at the same time, keeping her body close to his legs. She lowered herself slightly and let her breasts press down on his knees.

"Hold on, darling." He touched her cheek and stopped her "Tell me about this again, what media channels are we using here, is it just print?"

"No, Sir, this is all of them, print, TV and web." Kriti rested her left hand boldly on his thigh, while she pointed and moved the slides with her right hand.

"Isn't that very expensive?" Vikas asked, he didn't object to any of her moves.

"Yes, Sir." Kriti agreed "But this is the most aggressive strategy. I have other options in the next slides."

"Ok. Sorry, I interrupted. Go on, honey." He said.

"No problem, Sir." Kriti said. She continued with the presentation, leaving one hand on his thigh.

When she finished, he said "Excellent presentation. I like this girl," he told Jacqueline "she is very thorough."

He pulled her up by the hand. Kriti got up and as he pulled down, she lowered her butt on his left leg. A hot chill went up her spine as she rested her ass on his lap like that. The tablet was still in her hand.

"Okay, so tell me this," Vikas said, moving the tablet in her hand with his right hand so all three of them could see the tablet right side up "which one of these approaches do you recommend?"

"Sir, that will depend on which partner we go with in US." Jacqueline said.

Kriti put her right around his shoulders staying close to him "All approaches have their pros and cons, Sir, but we can choose one based on our timeline."

"Good. Very good prep work. You girls have done well." Vikas stood up and Kriti had to reluctantly stand as well. But he kept his arm around her waist which she liked.

"I think you are both handling this well, but keep in mind this is all just prep work for our expansion. You need to keep the current work going as well."

"Of course, Sir." Jacqueline said, she was keeping herself close to him as well "That will continue as usual. When can we meet again, Sir?"

"Umm, we have our usual PR department meeting on Friday, don't we?" He asked.

Kriti let Jacqueline answer that while she herself cuddled up to the boss as closely as she could. His arm around her waist and his hand resting on her bare belly felt like success to Kriti.

"No, Sir. Pari said for your first week back, she didn't want to overload your calendar." Jacqueline said.

"Alright, I will talk to Pari and see how Friday looks otherwise we'll have it early next week." Vikas said.

"Ok, Sir." Jacqueline said.

"Now tell me about this girl," he squeezed Kriti to him "what's her story?"

Jacqueline smiled "She's new in PR department, fresh meat. She's my junior and she's on probation for about two and a half months more."

"Cool." Vikas kept Kriti pressed to him as he looked at her "While your probation is going on you will be under my direct control. Your line manager will stay Shakti Kapoor but you will report to me, I will see all your output. Any problems?"

"In being under your direct control?" Kriti flashed her beautiful toothy grin "Not at all. I am excited. I would love to stay directly under you even after my probation."

"We will see about that." He slapped her ass and said "Now, both of you go play in your own department, I have work to do."

"Yes, Sir." Kriti grinned and rubbed her ass like it had hurt more than it did.

"Me too, Sir." Jacqueline turned and bent over, presenting her ass to him.

"Oh, you need much more than this." Vikas said and slapped her ass harder than he had spanked Kriti.

Both the girls were giggling as they left his cabin.

Chapter 8 – Kriti is Smitten

"You little bitch!" Jacqueline said with a grin as they walked to the lift "I saw how you were sucking up to him. For someone who didn't even want to follow his dress code you were getting in there pretty quickly."

"He is just…" Kriti grinned as well "let's say I fell under his spell. I am sure you are too."

"Still mad at me for telling you to change?"

Kriti shook her head "I am really thankful to you for making me change. I would have kicked myself later otherwise."

"Exactly!"

"Can I wear a shorter skirt? Is that allowed?"

Jacqueline said "Shorter than this?"

Kriti nodded "I have a really sexy nylon micromini that hugs my ass and looks damn hot."

"Wow, but will you dare to wear that without panties?"

"Oh yes," Kriti nodded "no panties for Kriti Sanon from now on."

"Yes, you can wear a shorter skirt, there's no limitation from HR side. Are you trying to tell him something?"

Kriti nodded "Just that I am available when he wants."

"I thought so." Jacqueline said, as she got into the lift "save that skirt for Friday though, you probably won't see him before then."

"Good idea." Kriti followed her in "Thanks."

"Just don't get in my way, I have been trying to get under him for a long time."

"Oh?" Kriti looked at her "I thought he was already banging you, the way you were almost in his lap…"

"No," Jacqueline shook her head "I wish. But I am making progress. He will claim me any day now, I can feel it."

"Good luck." Kriti said "I am your junior, please keep guiding me too."

"Sure." Jacqueline smiled.

Chapter 9 – Genelia's Gift

Genelia walked into the big boss' office "Sir, I have kept the packages in the café. Whenever you are ready, I will go with you and help you distribute them."

"Thank you, darling." Vikas got up "Come here, Gen."

She walked around his desk and approached with him with a racing heart "Yes, Sir."

"I got something for you, I don't want to give you this in front of everybody, they will be jealous." He took a box from his desk and handed it to Genelia.

"Oh, wow, thank you, Sir." She opened it. It was a silver necklace with a nice pendant.

"Sir, this is beautiful!" Genelia said excitedly "Can I hug you, Sir?"

"Will that be enough?" He pulled her to him and enclosed her in his arms "I mean I did carry it for you all the way from Thailand."

Genelia turned her face up and pressed her lips on his. He squeezed her in his arms and kissed her back. His tongue teased her bottom lip. Their breaths mingled in a hot, erotic mix. Genelia parted her lips, clearing the way for his tongue. He tasted her mouth with his tongue exploring deeper as the kiss grew hotter and more lustful. Genelia pressed her tits into his chest as she squeezed herself against him. His hand easily caressed her smooth, bare back up and down. Genelia had fantasised about kissing him many times, but this was the first time she was really experiencing it. She didn't want to stop sucking his tongue, but they both got completely breathless and Vikas gently pulled back.

"Thank you, Sir. For the necklace and for the…" Genelia blushed and left her sentence unfinished.

"You are welcome, sweetheart, for both." Vikas smiled "Now, shall we go down?"

He collected Parineeti also and they went down to the 10th floor. There was no conference hall in VisCom that could contain all of its 200-odd employees at one time and it did seem like they were all there. They filled the café, the corridor outside and the empty conference hall opposite the café. Vikas stood on a chair so he could be seen and heard all the way to the back.

"Good afternoon, all. It's wonderful to see you again." Vikas said "I have brought some chocolates and gifts for you." There was cheering "Don't get too excited, they are just some games, and showpieces and things like that. You didn't really think I would bring you cars and big screen TVs, did you?" People chuckled. "They are just to say that I missed you guys. No, it doesn't mean my honeymoon was boring. It was great, thank you very much." Some people laughed, some girls did "Whoo!" noises.

Vikas continued "Secondly, it's nice to see that you guys kept the company running smoothly and even better in my absence, makes me think I should go on at least one honeymoon a year." People laughed "And how do I know the company is running better, well here's the good news, we have been nominated for two awards, both in the best print ad and best TV categories."

There was very loud cheering and applause this time. Vikas waited for it to die down then continued "I wish I could take some of that credit but it's you guys, your hard work, your passion, your love for your craft that makes it possible. I am sure we will win but even if we don't, I just want to recognise that you guys are doing great work, and you should be proud of yourself. I know I am proud of you." Again, a long applause break. He spoke for another minute then left the support staff to distribute the gifts.

Chapter 10 – Meeting the HR Manager

"Hi Rani." Vikas said entering the HR manager's office "Hi Ravi, are you in trouble with HR again?"

The guy who looked the typical accountant and was in fact an accountant smiled "Please don't malign my character, Sir. I am never in trouble with HR. I actually came to ask Rani if we are hiring for any jobs. My wife needs a job."

"Rashmika needs a job?" Vikas said, taking a seat "Saving for that Ferrari, I am sure?"

"No Sir." Ravi laughed "We need to buy a house. Our landlord is selling the house where we live and we have to move out in the next two weeks. We actually put a deposit on a house and we were all set to move there but at the last moment, they have raised the EMI. We can't move unless we can raise more money. If Rashmika could find a job, we would be able to meet the EMI."

"What kind of job can she do?" Vikas asked.

Ravi said "That's the problem, Sir. She is not trained in anything specific. She used to do an office admin job before our marriage."

"Do we have anything like that?" Vikas looked at HR manager Rani Mukherjee.

"No, Sir. We are only hiring for the secretary pool right now, but Ravi says, she's not trained in that. Nobody does steno training these days but we need at least MS-Office experience."

"Hmmm." Vikas thought for a moment "Pari said she needs someone to help her sort out the backlog of paper files. I am sure Rashmika could do that, right?"

Rani said "Yes, Sir, that task doesn't need any special skill, but that role is only for two weeks, that's what Pari told me, at least."

Vikas looked at Ravi "Your need is pretty urgent, isn't it?"

"Yes," Ravi nodded "we will be homeless in two weeks."

"Sir," Rani interjected "that job is a temp job as an office assistant. I doubt that it will fulfil Ravi's need."

"Hmmm." Vikas thought then said "Rani, raise that position to Assistant Clerk that would be better paying. And extend it to one month." He turned to Ravi "This will allow you to get the house and move. Then we will think of a better solution in the month we have. How's that?"

"Can that be done?" Ravi looked from Vikas to Rani.

Rani nodded "When the big boss says it, it can always be done."

"That would be great. It would give me breathing space." Ravi said "Thank you, Sir. Thank you so much."

"You are most welcome." Vikas said "Now if you are done, I need to talk to Rani."

"Sure, Sir. Thank you, Sir." Ravi went out.

"Now, what am I going to do with you?" Vikas turned to Rani.

"With me or to me, Sir?" Rani flashed her sexy smile.

"See, again you are being so naughty. We send girls to HR for being naughty."

"Then good thing I am already here" Rani smiled even wider.

"And looking so damn hot." Vikas said.

"Why, thank you, Sir. Finally, you noticed." Rani said.

She was wearing a halter dress with a modern print. It was fitting tightly around her small, slender body and covered only up to her mid-thighs. Rani was gorgeous but not very tall. She did have great legs though, so she used them whenever possible. She also always wore high heels, even today she was wearing 8" high heels with 4" platforms.

 "Have you become more of a cocktease since I was gone?" Vikas said.

"I dressed for you today." Rani said petulantly "And you are calling me a cocktease. By the way you can only call a girl cocktease if she's not willing to follow through."

"And you are willing?"

"You know I am." Rani said meeting his gaze.

Rani Mukherjee had joined VisCom a couple of years ago as an HR executive. Her boss, Manas Batra, the HR Manager at that time, had fucked her in the interview and she had submitted like a good girl. After that he had kept her as his whore for one year until he left the company. Rani had met Vikas in an official HR meeting and she had given him strong hints in that meeting itself that if he wanted to bend her over his desk, he would not get any resistance from her side. But Vikas had not taken the offer. She had made the offer many times, more and more boldly as the time passed. .

After Manas had left for another company, Vikas had bypassed other senior HR exec's and promoted Rani to HR manager. Again she had made the offer, this time directly, that she would love to spread her legs for him. She even told him that she would like to work under his direct control. Vikas did work with her directly, interacting on a regular basis about work, but he had not fucked her. Rani had never stopped trying and always dressed sexy when she met him.

"Don't you have a conference area?" Vikas said. He knew she had an area with sofas and a coffee table behind a partition where they had had many meetings.

"Please come." Rani said and took him behind the partition. Vikas sat on a sofa and patted his thigh. Rani quickly walked to him and straddled him, her knees on the sofa on either side of him.

"Is this my lucky day?" She said as she put her hands on his shoulders and lowered her ass right down to his crotch. They had flirted a lot in the past but never been this intimate. He had never even kissed her.

"Didn't you always tell me you wanted to be in my direct control?" Vikas ran his hands slowly up and down her sides. His fingertips brushing lightly on her bare back.

"I still do." Rani said, leaning in closer "You control HR and work closely with me on that but that's not what I meant. I wanted to be personally under your control and still do."

Vikas untied her halter strap and pulled her dress down, baring her tits. Rani gasped. She had lovely, nicely proportioned tits for her small, slender body. He took one breast in his hand and fondled it slowly.

Rani moaned "Are you really going to take me under your control? You won't be a tease now, will you?"

He smiled and leaned in, closing his mouth around her hardening nipple, he sucked her breast and teased her nipple with his tongue making it harder. Rani pushed her fingers into hair and pressed his head into her breast.

"Mmmmm, God." She squirmed on his lap "Yes, please, boss. Yes. Take me in your possession, Sir."

Vikas caressed her cheek, brushing her hair from her face "You always wanted to work under my direct control. Let's make that happen."

"Oh yes, Sir!" She leaned in and kissed his neck "Yes, please do, Sir."

He unzipped his pants and pulled out his cock. It was already almost fully hard. Rani felt it hot and meaty under her and started to rub on it. Vikas pushed her short dress up higher over her hips. He grabbed her ass cheeks and placed her right over his cockhead. Rani moaned as his cockhead rubbed in her pussy hole. She started to push down but his cockhead was too big for her tight hole and it deflected. Vikas reached down and held his long, hard shaft in his hand.

"Now, take it in." He whispered in her ear. Rani started moving down again and whimpered when she found that it was stretching her tight pussy too wide. Her husband was nowhere that big and her pussy was not used to having such a thick cock in it. Vikas pushed with his hips and his cockhead entered her tight cunt, followed by two more massive inches of his meaty beast. Rani yelped like a kicked dog.

"Ah!" She cried out and lowered her head on Vikas' shoulder. She was panting as she tried to bear the pain of his throbbing beast stuffing her so tight.

"You ok, baby?" He whispered in her ear and kissed her neck.

"Mhmmm, yes, Sir." She moaned "My husband is not that big, Sir. I knew you would hurt inside me, I just didn't know how much."

He fondled her soft, full tits and kissed her cheek "This is just the first time, hon. We will make it a regular activity and train you fully."

"God, I would love that, Sir." Rani pushed down taking more of his huge cock inside her and whimpered again as it conquered fresh territory in her.

The feeling she was getting of being completely under his control and at his mercy was turning Rani on much more than the pain was holding her back. She started moving her ass up and down, fucking herself on his throbbing, hard cock. He rubbed her smooth back up and down, feeling her soft skin under his hands. Rani had flirted with him so many times, and given him the offer so often that she was finding it unbelievable that today he was finally in her. She had had dreams like that before. Most of her fantasies that she visualised when she fucked her husband were related to him banging her on his desk or coming into her office and fucking her right on her desk. The long wait and the anticipation of him owning her from now on was creating an immense excitement in her body and Rani was feeling like she was about to explode any moment.

"It feels wonderful, Sir." She moaned in his ear "Finally you are in me. It's a dream come true."

He lifted his hand and slapped her tight, bare ass, making it sting "Spread those legs wider, baby, sink down lower."

She did as he ordered and then yelped when that made his cockhead hit her cervix. The pain that shot off from her cunt all the way up into her body and towards her extremities made Rani completely helpless in his arms. Vikas grabbed her ass cheeks and bounced her on his cock. Rani felt the temperature in her body rising. Her yelps became faster and louder. And then her pussy exploded.

Rani felt like a massive truck had hit her and spun her around. She could feel her whole body trembling, supercharged, electrified. She could see stars and yet she was still on his cock riding him like a hungry, wanton slut. He kept her in his grip and drilled her cunt harder and faster. She kept cumming on his cock, soaking his meaty shaft with her cunt juices. She knew her screams were too loud but she had no control over them. She had no control over anything anymore. The sensations of pleasure were like bright points of electric lights inside her that heated her up to bright red then slowly cooled down through the whole spectrum of colours. She could not count how many of these points were alive in her at one point, but they seemed to twinkle off and new ones generated every few milliseconds.

"Oh mumma," She whispered in his ear "you killed me. You killed me, I died and went to heaven." Her body was slightly cooler now and she felt that she could speak.

He kissed her cheek and bit her earlobe.

"It proves one thing." Rani said again.

"What's that?" Vikas was keeping her on his cock, fucking her with slower, but deep strokes.

"All this time I was chasing you, wanting to be your little whore in the office," Rani said, looking into his eyes "and I was right. I was totally right in wanting it."

"Do you still want to be my whore?"

"I hope that I am your whore now, Sir." She said "Totally available to you and ready for you to fuck when you want."

He smiled "As I said, we will make it a regular activity."

"That would be amazing for me! Oh by the way, Sir, I hired a new assistant for me."

"And why are you telling me this now while you are riding my cock?" He smiled.

"Because she's a hot piece of ass. I want to introduce her to you when she joins. She's hot, young and fuckable. You will like her."

"What if I do like her? What then?"

"Then you will fuck her and take into your possession." Rani said "I won't be the only thing under your direct control. The HR department will be under your direct control."

"Hmmm, it has a certain twisted pleasure in it that appeals to the monster in me."

"And to the monster in me, Sir?" Rani smiled as she squeezed his thick cock with her pussy muscles.

Vikas spanked her ass, making it sting where his calloused hand landed on her bare skin.

"Show me that whore side of you, Rani." He said "Why should I own you? Show me."

Rani yelped as he slapped her soft, firm ass several times and rode his cock harder. She rose to his challenge and pushed down until his cockhead was pushing on her cervix and fucked herself incredibly deep on his large, powerful cock.

"Mmmmm, that's like a good whore." He said in her ear and spanked her ass again. Rani was encouraged and motivated by this to ride his cock even harder, but just then her pussy exploded and she lost control on her body again. She tried to keep riding him but her movements were erratic and jerky now. Her moans were telling the story of her arousal. Vikas grabbed her ass cheeks and laid her on the sofa, without letting his cock out of her cunt.

Then he nailed her hard into the sofa, using forceful, deep strokes to rip her cunt open with his massive cock and teach her where she belonged. Rani was sure she was about to die under him, but fortunately, just then she felt him explode inside her. The heat from his cum flooding her womb warmed her whole body and she felt like every cell of her skin was on fire. Vikas continued to drill her cunt, fucking her expertly while he dumped his load into her and claimed her as his whore.

She clung to him with both arms, squeezing herself against his hard, manly body, showing him how much she loved being broken in by him. Vikas kept his dick inside her and pumped her with smooth, deep strokes that were not that rough now. She kissed him and sucked his tongue while he fucked her smoothly with his pulsating beast. Rani ran her hands up and down his back. She rubbed his neck and kissed him intimately, swallowing his saliva. After a long, incredibly sexy kiss, they parted. Vikas slowly pulled out of Rani's cunt. She moaned as her pussy felt the loss of his throbbing beast.

He guided her down to the floor as he sat on the sofa. She knelt between his feet and looked up at him with a smile "A boss should always own the girls under him. I am so glad that you finally took charge of me."

Vikas smiled and watched her beautiful face as she licked his cock clean. He stroked her head and she responded like a pet bitch.

When Vikas left, Rani went to fix her appearance. She was smiling widely.

Chapter 11 – Pujita Acts with Boldness

"Puji, I need to hurry or I will miss my local. Are you not going yet?" Genelia said.

"Well, he hasn't left yet." Pujita said "I will wait a little bit more."

"Honey, you know he can work as late as he wants. He's the CEO and he has his car. Don't you have your local to catch?"

"It's okay. I will wait a little bit more."

"Sure. Your choice." Genelia said and again fingered her new necklace "I am so gonna wear a deep-neck dress tomorrow."

Pujita was openly jealous of her gift from the big boss that they both had a crush on. "You lucky bitch, I bet you will wear it every day now."

"Of course. It's from Him!" Genelia said.

Genelia wanted to brag some more but she had one eye on the clock as well. She left before she could risk missing the train.

Not even ten minutes had passed before Pujita heard the lift come down. She looked over and saw Vikas stepping out. She stood up and smoothed her dress down. She was wearing a pink, sleeveless, deep-neck, silk minidress that showed her lovely breasts in a ridiculously sexy visual. It was tight around her curvy body and had been attracting attention all day. The boss had noticed it in the morning which had thrilled Pujita.

"Still here, darling?" Vikas said walking up to the reception counter. Instead of going around to the front, he walked in behind the counter and right to Pujita. She smiled "How can I go when my boss is still working?" She tried to sound like she worked directly under him even though they both knew there was no connection.

"That's sweet." Vikas grinned "But I am a bad example. Don't follow my lead in this."

Pujita changed the topic "Sir…can I ask you something?"

"Anything." He said.

"Sir…I don't want to sound like a brat but…I mean…" She hesitate then decided to just blurt it out "Sir, how come Genelia got a special gift from you and I just got chocolate?"

Vikas smiled and stepped closer to her "Because she came to my office and you didn't. I didn't want to send your gift via her."

He pulled out a little gift box from his briefcase and handed it to her.

"Oh my god!" Pujita was suddenly overwhelmed. She tore into the package and took out a box. Inside was a silver necklace, but instead of a design like Genelia's pendant this one had the letter "P" in it, with sparkling rhinestones on it.

"I love it!" She said.

"May I?" He took it from her. Pujita turned around and held her hair up. Vikas put the necklace around her neck and clasped it. Then leaned in and kissed her neck. She moaned softly.

As he pulled back, she turned to face him.

"Wow, thank you so much, Sir." She gushed "It looks great."

Vikas took the necklace in his fingers and let his hand move slowly up and down along its chain. The back of his fingers rubbed Pujita's smooth, warm breasts which were partially exposed in the deep neck dress.

"I agree." He said boldly caressing her tits with the back of his fingers.

"Sir, may I thank you properly for it?" Pujita asked with a racing heart.

"Oh, I like the sound of that."

Pujita stepped in close and hugged him like she had done in the morning but this time instead of kissing his cheek she boldly pressed her lips to his. Instead of pulling back, he squeezed her soft, supple body in his strong arms. Her full, soft tits got crushed on his chest and Pujita felt her pussy pulsing strongly at his closeness. She parted her lips to signal to him that he could do more with her if he wanted. He took her invitation and licked her bottom lip as he slipped his tongue into her mouth. Pujita welcomed it with her tongue, licking from below, helping him go deeper in her mouth.

The kiss was just as hot as it was inappropriate. The CEO kissing the married receptionist was not really as per the business manual but Pujita had lusted after him for so long that she was not going to miss this chance. She pressed her soft, warm body against him and sucked his tongue into her mouth, telling him that he could do with her what he wanted.

After a long and sexually charged kiss, Vikas pulled back and smiled "Damn! You do know how to thank a guy properly. You should thank me everyday."

"I won't mind, Sir." Pujita said in a sultry voice.

He smiled "Let's explore that later. For now, I need to go and you should go home too."

"Yes, Sir." Pujita had an idea "Sir, could you give me a lift? Just a couple of stations, so I don't have change trains?"

"That's fine, hon. I can drop you wherever you want." Vikas said "Are you ready to go?"

Pujita was so excited she almost left her stuff behind "Yes, Sir. Thank you, Sir."

She quickly picked up her bag and followed him out. Now her pussy was really throbbing.

Her pussy only got hotter and wetter when she sat next to him in the back seat of his Mercedes. Her short dress rode up as she sat down. She didn't pull it down. Instead she parted her legs.

As the driver got them into the Bombay traffic, Pujita leaned in and whispered to Vikas "I feel like thanking you again, Sir."

Vikas looked at her and raised his eyebrows. She bit her lip and nodded. He turned towards her. She turned her face up and they kissed. This time Pujita was more relaxed and sure of herself. She used her tongue to tease his lips, then licked between them. His breath was warming her cheek and it was making her heartbeat get faster. His hands caressed up her sides, feeling her soft, warm body in the tight, thin dress.

Pujita decided to be bold. She took his hand and placed it on her breast. Vikas fondled it slowly, then as the kiss got hotter and more passionate, his fingers closed around her breast and squeezed it harder. She moaned in his mouth and pressed herself more into him. Her dress was very deep cut. Vikas pushed his fingers inside and cupped her soft breast in his hand. She could feel the electricity flowing from his hand through her nipple into her body. She dared to reach down and rub his thigh. Then feeling bold, she moved her hand and felt his hard, long cock through the pants. It sent a chill down her spine to feel how big it was.

It was unbelievably hot for Pujita to be making out with her boss that she had lusted after for so long. When they got to her place, she was sorry that they had not got stuck in a traffic jam tonight. She kissed him again and thanked him then she had to go home. That night her husband got lucky when Pujita said she wanted to have sex. He didn't know that she was thinking about her boss the whole time she was fucking him.

Chapter 12 – Family Reunion at Sonali's

"Hi Jiju!" Rhea chirped as soon as Vikas entered the house, completely ignoring Kajal who was also with him.

Vikas smiled "Hi hon."

Rhea boldly pressed in for a hug and kissed him on the lips. Vikas let her without kissing back too hard or making it a French kiss. Kajal simply ignored it and walked ahead into the living room. Rhea kept her arm around Vikas as she escorted him in a moment later.

"Jiju, take a seat, I will get you some water." Rhea said.

"Hi Amisha, you are also here?" Vikas said "Anything special going on?"

Amisha smiled and hugged him "No, we were just missing the family and we heard you and Kajal were coming over so I came too. Shriya is also here. Hemant will come here directly from his work. Prakash is working late but he will try to make it."

"Lovely family reunion then. Love it!"

Vikas sat down on the big sofa. Kajal hugged Amisha then knelt down and started to untie Vikas' shoe. Rhea came in with a glass of water on a tray. She put the tray on the coffee table, knelt down beside Kajal and started to untie Vikas' other shoe.

"What are you doing?" Kajal said.

"Same as what you are doing, taking Jiju's shoes off so he can relax." Rhea said.

"But I am his wife, I do this every day." Kajal said.

"Lucky bitch!" Rhea muttered.

"Hey!" Kajal protested.

"Oops, sorry di, you are my senior wife, I should be respectful." Rhea said "I apologise."

"Senior wife?" Kajal said "And you are my junior wife?"

"Yes, remember saali aadhi gharwali? I am his second wife. He will tell you himself but he is busy watching TV."

Vikas was listening to this all but staying out of it. He just smiled because the TV was off.

"Well, that way Amisha would be his half-wife too." Kajal said.

"I won't mind," Amisha said "but Vikas doesn't need an old model with lots of mileage. Rhea can serve him better."

"See, everybody is with the program, except you, dear sister." Rhea said to Kajal.

"Okay, if you are the junior wife, then put his shoes in my bedroom and bring his slippers." Kajal handed her the shoes and socks.

"Yes, di." Rhea took the shoes and went away smiling.

"Everyday she gets more out of hand." Kajal said.

"Can you blame her?" Amisha said "Who wouldn't fall in love with a man like that? You yourself did."

"Yes, but I married him." Kajal said.

"And she is his saali." Amisha said "You better get ready to share, she is very determined."

"That's what I am worried about." Kajal sighed "Where's mom?"

Sonali entered just then. "So lovely to have everybody together. Rhea was really missing you all and I must say I was, too."

"Hi Sasu Maa," Vikas said "where is Guddu?"

"On his way." Sonali said "He went for an interview. He is trying to find a job."

Kajal said "Patidev, should I show the photos?"

"Yes, darling." He pulled out a fat envelope from his briefcase and handed it to Kajal.

"How did you get the photos made so quickly?" Sonali said "I just told Rhea this afternoon which photos to send for printing."

"Ah, Sasu Maa," Vikas got up and took her shoulders in his hands "my sweet, simple Sasu Maa. It only takes a minute to print a photo these days and we have photo printers in my office. You might not know this, but I don't always wait for your daughters to tell me what to do."

"No, that's not what I mean." Sonali said "I was…"

"I know, Sasu Maa, I am just teasing you." Vikas kissed her cheek "You guys see the photos, I will just go change.

Rhea came back into the room and jumped with joy at seeing the photos in Kajal's hand.

Vikas looked at Amisha. She raised her eyebrows. He jerked his head ever so slightly. Then he left the room and went to Kajal's bedroom. A moment later Amisha followed him in.

Vikas closed the door behind her. He reached under the back of his coat and pulled out a similar but thinner envelope. He handed this to Amisha. Amisha opened it and pulled out the photos from it. She spread them on the bed. They were her photos from the private shoot that Vikas had done in Thailand. She looked very sexy in Vikas' shirt and nothing else.

"Wow, they look amazing!" Amisha gushed "You are such a great photographer."

"You can give yourself some credit too." Vikas said "Give yourself…13% of the credit."

"Oh my god!" Amisha looked at last photos which her of her completely nude with the shirt blowing back in the wind "You made me look so hot!"

"Again, I didn't have to try very hard. You are a damn hot babe." Vikas said, smiling "I was actually tempted to keep a copy of those last ones."

Looking from the photos, Amisha came close to him and hugged him tight. She kissed him on the cheek.

"You keep all the copies you want. I would be flattered that you did. But whenever you want a live preview, you only have to say."

"Really?"

"Any time. In fact…" Amisha stepped back and reached behind her. She was wearing a simple dress that reached almost to her knees. She undid the hooks and dropped the dress on the bed. Her bra and panties joined the dress in another minute.

She stood fully naked in front of her brother-in-law and opened her legs shoulder width.

"If you notice, completely smooth." She indicated her completely shaved pussy. Her pussy slit was glistening with slight moisture "And I will always keep it smoothly shaved from now on when I know that you can tell me to show it all at any time."

"I can?" Vikas asked innocently, but his eyes were taking in the beautiful sight. Amisha's big, heavy boobs, sagging slightly on her chest, her long legs, and yes, her bare, tight, smoothly shaved pussy. His eyes were surveying everything.

"You can. Any time." Amisha turned to show him her firm, tight ass then turned back to face him and smiled "With or without camera."

"Nice to know."

Again Amisha came to him and hugged him. She pressed her warm, naked body against him and turned her face up. Pressing her soft, plump lips on his lips she kissed him slowly and fully. Vikas tried not to respond at first but her warm, naked body was too much for any man to resist. He closed his arms around her and squeezed her tight. Her big, firm tits pressed on his chest. He tilted his head sideways and kissed her back hard. Amisha quickly opened her mouth, Vikas licked her lower lip and slipped his tongue into her mouth. His hands roamed over her naked back, moving down towards her sexy, well-rounded ass. Amisha pressed into him shamelessly and let her hot, bare pussy grind on his crotch. She moaned as she felt his hands squeezing her tight ass cheeks.

Vikas opened his arms and let her out when he felt that the kiss was becoming too passionate and wild. Amisha stepped back and caught her breath. Her pussy was glistening more now.

"I know I can't be a model now," She went back to standing in front of the photos, still breathing heavy "but you made me feel so sexy and glamorous. I love them. I will cherish them forever."

"Not that you can't be a model," Vikas corrected "but yes, you don't want to introduce casting couch into a marriage. It's not good."

"But if I had to…" Amisha asked haltingly "do you think, I could…I could still pass casting couch?"

Vikas ran his hanky on his lips and smiled "I think you will be even better on it now than when you were younger."

Stepping closer to him again, Amisha placed her hand on his chest and looked up into his eyes "If I were going to be a model, I would want you to train me for the casting couch, taking all the time you needed.”

He grinned and slapped her tight ass lightly “You are a naughty girl, Amisha. I am sure you’d have fit perfectly with the slutty girls in modelling.”

Giving a little fake moan at his slap, Amisha reached up and kissed his lips briefly.

“Thank you so much. I love them and I love you for doing this.” Amisha said “And thank you for not showing these to anyone else.”

“You are welcome.” Vikas told her “I will go back to the living room, you take your time. Enjoy!”

Amisha gave him a smile as he stepped out and closed the door behind him.

Chapter 13 – Quick Kitchen Visit

"Wow, look at you pretending to be a normal housewife." Vikas said as he entered the kitchen.

"I am a normal housewife, Vikas." Shriya laughed happily as she turned.

"Good. I am glad you left the whore in Thailand." He grinned, taking another step into the kitchen, not touching her at all.

She walked up to him "I will always be your whore on demand, Vikas."

He pulled her away from the door into the other corner and slipped his arm around her bare midriff. She was wearing a backless halter blouse and a thin saree. She pressed her soft body tightly into him as she kissed him. Vikas rubbed her smooth, bare back, rubbing her soft skin while her braless tits pressed on his chest. He licked and sucked her lips, teasing her bottom lip before pushing his tongue into her mouth. Shriya pressed close and drank his saliva as she sucked his tongue.

Vikas let his left hand slide down to her butt and kneaded her tight ass cheeks hard in the thin saree. She started to grind her pussy hungrily into his crotch. Her breath was already heavy and her heart was beating faster. She shamelessly humped his cock through the clothes and moaned into his mouth. Vikas squeezed and kneaded her soft body in his strong hands. He treated her body like it belonged to him and played with her boldly. She responded to his touches and squeezes wantonly with a craving that showed in her moans and her grinding hips.

They broke the breathless kiss and Shriya hugged him tightly. Her whole body was pressing against his strong, manly frame and Shriya was rubbing herself on him like she wanted him to fuck her through the clothes.

"Oh god, when will you fuck me, Vikas?" She whispered in his ear.

"Well, our deal was that I will nail you when we have an opportunity." Vikas reminded her "So, we'll just have to wait for that."

They heard the sound of the living room door opening and Shriya got out of his embrace. They heard the sound of footsteps through the dining room. A minute later, when Sonali entered the kitchen Vikas was standing next to Shriya and saying "Won't it get cold by the time we have dinner if you make it now?"

Shriya said "No, Vikas. This is saag, it will take a couple of hours to cook on the slow fire."

"Oh, I see." Vikas said "Hello Sasu Maa. Did you like any of the photos?"

"They are very nice, Damad ji." Sonali said "Bahu, I was thinking…"

"Ji mummy ji?" Shriya said.

"In Thailand you gave Damad ji a massage." Sonali said.

"Yes, I did." Shriya said cautiously. She didn't know where her saas was going with this.

"Well, that was just vacation, but Vikas works so hard, he must get a lot of stress. Maybe you could give him a massage from time to time."

Shriya smiled "I would be happy to, mummy ji. Vikas knows that I am always available for him."

"No, no, just being available is not enough, Bahu," Sonali said "He takes care of everybody except himself. He will never ask. You need to make a plan and make sure he keeps to it."

"Ji mummy, ji. I will take care of it." Shriya said.

Chapter 14 – Vikas Rules Family Dinner

Hemant and Prakash both arrived before dinner so it was a full table. When Vikas came back after washing his hands, everybody had already sat down, only Sonali and Shriya were bringing some dishes from the kitchen. As usual, the place at the head of the table had been left for Vikas. He took his place and said "It's different from the first class dining room on the ship but it's great to be eating with family again."

"Yes, but the ship was a lot of fun." Guddu said "Bombay feels boring after Thailand."

"It feels boring to you?" Shriya said as she brought the last dish and sat down next to him "You don't know how boring it is to wear saree after getting used to wearing dresses all the time."

"The courier will be here this week, I think." Vikas said "There are quite a few of your dresses in that."

"Oh good. I am going to start wearing them." Shriya said.

"Yes, you should." Vikas agreed "You are young, you have a beautiful figure, there's no need to dress like an aunty jee. It's bad enough that I can't get Sasu maa to dress more modern."

"I am old and I live in a middle class society." Sonali said "But Shriya, you should wear dresses, your area is quite modern, isn't it?"

"Well, it's kind of ok." Shriya said.

"Mumma, you are not so old." Rhea said "Fashion is what keeps a person young."

"At least listen to her," Vikas said "she is an expert in fashion."

Rhea beamed.

Sonali changed the topic "Damad ji, there was something I wanted to ask about. Rhea and Guddu have been asking that we should get a cable connection, but I am not in favour. I think it has a very corrupting influence on growing children. What do you think?"

"Hmmm," Vikas thought for a moment "Sasu Maa, corrupting things are everywhere. The world is full of them. When we went to Malaysia and Thailand, there were a whole lot of corrupting things there. I knew about it but I still took the family. I think the answer is not to close your children off from everything that may corrupt them but to teach them the values that will help them decide what influences to accept and which ones to stay away from."

"Ji, Damad ji." Sonali said.

"I think you have raised children who are smart enough and strong enough to know the difference. I see no harm in getting a cable connection."

"Yay!" Guddu rejoiced.

"Thank you, Jiju," Rhea said "not for the cable but what you said. You are such a wise man. That's why everybody loves you."

"I agree, Damad ji." Sonali said "I had not thought about it like that. My children are smart and I can trust them to make good choices."

"Happy to help." Vikas said.

The dinner continued in a fun family manner. They had so much to talk about from the trip. The dessert was kheer (rice pudding) made by Shriya.

"Wonderful kheer, Shriya." Vikas said "Best I have ever had."

Shriya blushed "Thank you, Vikas."

"My wife doesn't make good kheer." Vikas said.

"Oh really?" Kajal said "I have never made kheer since we have been married."

"See, doesn't even care enough to make kheer for me." Vikas lamented.

"What are you doing?" Kajal asked suspiciously "Are you trying to pick a fight with me?"

"Babe," Vikas said in a stage whisper "after marriage the husband is expected to complain about his wife. I am trying to fit in so people will accept me as a normal husband."

Kajal laughed "You are never a normal husband, dear. You are extra-ordinary."

"I second that." Rhea said.

"I third that." Shriya added.

Prakash said "I call this meeting of the Vikas Fan Club to order."

"Hold on." Amisha said "We don't have quorum yet."

"We only need 10% for quorum, you are here, Shriya is here, and Kajal and Rhea. We have 100% attendancc." Prakash said.

"No, we don't. We are missing many people." Amisha insisted.

"Like?" Hemant asked this time.

Amisha said "Like all the staff of the first class on the ship, like the people whose property Vikas saved from the thieves, like the captain of the ship, like the woman whose necklace Vikas saved…"

Shriya added "Like his whole office. I saw those girls, and guys. Every one of them was a fan of their boss. You don't see that often."

"Well, my office staff loves me, too." Prakash said.

"Not like this." Amisha said "Your staff is more afraid of you. It's not the same thing."

"You forgot me." Guddu said "I am in Jiju's fan club too."

"Me too." Sonali said and smiled.

"Oh, I am so embarrassed," Vikas said dramatically "someone change the subject, please."

"Would you like more kheer, Vikas?" Shriya said.

"No, darling. I am good. It was wonderful but I am already too full. Thank you." Vikas said.

"You are welcome."

"Damad ji, Rhea was asking to go to her college function." Sonali asked as she saw an opening.

Vikas looked at Rhea "What function is this, baby?"

"Jiju, new semester is starting, so there's Welcome Freshers party." Rhea said.

"Is the college giving this?" Vikas asked.

"No, it's by the student union, in a club."

"Will there be the same crowd as last time, at your annual function?"

"Yes, I think so, jiju."

"Then, no, I don't want you to go." Vikas said softly but definitely.

"Okay, jiju." Rhea said.

"What?" Sonali challenged "You ate half my brain for permission to go to that party! And now you are ok to not go?"

"No, mumma, jiju is right, it's not safe. I am sorry I bothered you so much about it."

Sonali's jaw dropped "I can't believe this is the same girl who's been hounding me to go to this party for almost a week! She chewed my ear on the whole flight."

Rhea said "Sorry, mumma, I did not think it through. What jiju says is right."

Vikas said "I can't go with you, darling, and I don't want you to go alone."

"I understand, jiju." Rhea said easily "You are absolutely right. I partied so much with you on your honeymoon. This is nothing compared to that."

"Well, we can party again soon." Vikas suggested "Remember our club date?"

"Really?" Rhea looked excited "Just you and me?"

"Well…." Vikas hesitated "How about take my wife as well?"

"You mean your first wife." Rhea corrected "I am the second, obviously."

"Obviously!" Shriya said, grinning.

Vikas smiled "Yes, my first wife" he pointed at Kajal, then at Rhea "and my second wife. Is that ok?"

"Sure. I can live with that." Rhea said "I suppose I have to share you with her."

"Hey!" Kajal interjected "If anything, I am sharing him with you."

"Yay!" Rhea clapped "She said she's ready to share you, jiju."

"Oh, you tricked me!" Kajal said.

Vikas grinned.

"Can we come too?" Guddu asked.

"Obviously not!" Rhea said before Vikas could speak.

"Sorry bro," Vikas lifted his hands "it's Rhea's party."

Hemant said "Rhea shouldn't be partying. We should be thinking about her marriage."

"I will cut anybody who talks about my marriage." Rhea picked up a butter knife and pointed it at Hemant.

"Ok, ok." Hemant lifted his hands in surrender "I won't. Calm down, jhaansi ki rani!"

Rhea put the knife down and said "If you guys want to talk about marriage, talk about Guddu, he's older than me."

"Hey! What did I do to you?" Guddu said "Anyway, I need to settle down first. I don't even have a job yet."

"So, your B.Sc. is finished?" Vikas asked.

"B. Tech., jiju, and yes, I graduated this year. Now I am looking for a job."

"In IT?" Vikas asked.

"Yes, jiju, I want to go into software development."

"Sasu Maa said you had an interview today." Vikas said "How did it go?"

"Not good, Jiju. They are looking for experienced people." Guddu said "How will I ever get experience if nobody gives me a job?"

"Hmmm, remind me after dinner. I will give you a number. Mr. Rajesh Vadhwa, he's a general manager in TCS. He will find you a role in his company or refer you to someone else."

"Wow, TCS!" Guddu asked "How do you know him, jiju?"

"Old friend. We were in MBA together."

"Thank you, jiju. Wow, TCS!"

"Sasu Mass, I was thinking," Vikas said "all that land to the left of the door is just being wasted. You know the open area on the left hand as we enter? There is an old broken-down toilet there that nobody uses, and in the rain that open land just collects water. Why don't we use it?"

"I have thought about it often, Damad ji," Sonali said "but it would be very expensive to get that built up. This house is enough for our living needs, so I never really tried planning anything for it."

"Well, I would like to put that to good use." Vikas said "Would you mind?"

"Of course not." Sonali said "You can decide to use it as you like."

Rhea said "What are you thinking, jiju?"

"Please a home theatre, jiju." Guddu said.

"Yeah, so you can watch more TV." Amisha said.

"Shut up, children." Sonali said "Let him speak. What Damad ji decides will happen."

"I am thinking there is space enough for three rooms there." Vikas said "We could make a game room, a gym and a workshop for Rhea where she can make her dresses."

"Oh my god!" Rhea stood up in excitement "That is so amazing, I didn't even think about it."

She came over to Vikas and hugged him "See, mumma, he thinks of both his wives, not just one."

"Of course, he's a good husband." Sonali smiled.

"But jiju, after marriage, I will live with you," Rhea said with a glint in her eye "what will happen of the workshop?"

"I don't know nothing about marriage or living arrangements" Vikas lifted his hands and pointed to Kajal "you have to talk to my senior wife about that. But let me ask you this, do you plan to do a job as a fashion designer or start your own business?"

"Well, I would like to do business, Jiju, but that's not easy, or cheap, so I may need to do job first to get some field experience and save some money."

"That's perfectly fine then. When you start your business, the workshop will shift to your proper workshop and we'll put a cot in that room where Guddu can sleep on then nights when his wife kicks him out."

Guddu's mouth fell open at this unprovoked attack and everybody burst into laughter.

"Damad ji, can we put a massage table in one of the rooms where Shriya can give you a massage from time to time?" Sonali said.

"I don't need a table, mummy jee," Shriya said "bed works fine for massage."

"You are sweet, honey," Vikas said "but I don't really need a massage like Sasu Mass seems to think. I don't get that much stress."

"And we can take him out for a Thai massage if he needs it." Prakash interjected.

"God, no!" Vikas said "Thai massage is hard, man. I don't know how you guys handled it. I had one and I was sore for two days."

"Oh, it's alright." Hemant said.

"Shall we see the photos from the trip?" Rhea said, bored with the topic.

This prompted everybody to finally get up from the dinner table.

Chapter 15 – Vikas Chilling with Family

Hemant looked at some pictures then went to see an old friend of his who lived nearby. The other family members looked at the photos and discussed the memories related to them.

"Rhea looks so pretty." Amisha said to Vikas "Look how good she looks in a bikini."

"Yes, she's really beautiful. But you look good yourself." He handed her a picture "See. Looks like you still got it."

Amisha looked at the photo but didn't say anything. She was deep in thought, remembering the day Vikas had taken those pictures.

"I need to tidy up the kitchen." Sonali said and got up. Shriya went to help her.

When Shriya came back to the living room, Vikas was watching TV sitting on the floor with his back to the sofa and Rhea was sitting between his legs, practically in his lap. He had his right leg bent at the knee so she was not sitting right against his crotch but her back was resting on his chest and he had one arm around her midriff. Rhea's head was resting back on his shoulder.

"Vikas, why are you sitting on the floor?" Shriya said "Sit on the sofa, na?"

"No, sweetheart, I sit in the chair all day, it is tiring. Sitting on the floor feels better for my back right now." Vikas said.

"Aww, you poor dear." Shriya "Come, let me massage you."

"It's ok, Shriya. I am not in pain or anything." Vikas said "Let me watch the movie."

"You can keep watching the movie." Shriya said and came over "Just make space so I can sit behind you."

She sat on the sofa with him between her legs and started to massage his head and shoulders. He could feel her soft legs pressing lightly against his body. She was wearing a long, thin nightie and he could feel her soft warmth through it. In a minute, Vikas could smell the faint smell of her pussy as she continued to massage his shoulders.

Rhea turned her head and said softly in his ear "Jiju, let me know if I become too heavy for you."

Vikas smiled and kissed lightly just below her jaw "You are not heavy, my love, but I will tell you when I need to change positions."

She placed her hand on his hand and happily went back to watching the movie.

When Sonali came into the room a little later, she saw Shriya massaging Vikas from the sofa. She came over to Shriya and stroked her head "Good girl. That's what I was saying." Shriya smiled and continued to massage Vikas.

Hemant came back pretty drunk after hanging out with his friend. Nobody seemed to be surprised. Shriya knew they would have to stay there overnight so she had already changed into a nightie. Only Prakash was offended that Hemant had not taken him drinking with him.

That seemed to mark the end of the evening. Everybody decided to go to bed. It was a normal custom at Sonali's to have warm milk before sleep. She went to the kitchen while Guddu and Prakash supported Hemant and helped him to his room. Amisha went to say goodnight to her mother as they were going home.

Rhea said goodnight to Vikas with a kiss on his lips. This time both Kajal and Shriya saw it but both overlooked it. After Rhea went to her room, Kajal and Shriya went to help Sonali. Vikas went to Kajal's bedroom and changed into pyjamas that he had started keeping there now.

Chapter 16 – Stolen Kisses

A few minutes later Shriya came in with a glass of milk. She put it on the side table and asked Vikas "Do you need anything else?"

Vikas pulled open the sash that was holding her nightie together and pulled her down on the bed. He pressed his hot lips on her lips and kissed her fully. She placed her hand behind his head and kissed him back eagerly. She was not wearing a bra, so when Vikas moved his hand down inside her open nightie, his fingers touched her soft, bare breast. He kneaded it slowly as he sucked her lips.

"I have not locked the door." She panted as he lifted off her after a hot kiss.

"Where is Kajal?"

"Helping mummy jee in the kitchen." She said.

"Ok." He pressed his mouth around her nipple and sucked her breast into his mouth. Shriya gasped as the hot sensations flooded her body and set her pussy on fire. She squirmed under him as he boldly played with her gorgeous body. He left one breast and started sucking on the other. Shriya's body was thrashing on the body. His mouth on her breast and his hand kneading the other breast, she was feeling her whole body get burning hot within a minute. She wanted his dick in her even though she knew it was not the right time or place.

"Not enough time to nail you." Vikas said softly, as he looked at her gorgeous face flushed with sexual excitement.

She shook her head "No, but please take me soon."

He nodded and picked up the glass of milk.

"I should go." She got up and tied up her nightie.

When he finished the milk, she took the glass and kissed his lips once quickly before slipping out the door.

Sonali was tidying up the kitchen while Kajal was washing the dishes from the milk. Shriya put Vikas' glass in the sink and started to help out.

"I was really pleased to see that you took my advice, bahu." Sonali said "Vikas takes care of all of us. It's not just Kajal's job, we all need to make sure he is happy. You, Kajal, Amisha, all should take care of him. Amisha lives far, but you live close to us and Vikas' place both. You need to make sure you take care of him."

"Of course, mummy ji, I understand." Shriya said.

Kajal said "Bhabhi is very intelligent, mummy. She knows we all need to serve him well and keep him happy."

Shriya nodded "Definitely, I think of it even more important than serving my husband. Vikas is very important to our family and I am happy to do whatever necessary."

It was not very clear to Shriya what her mother-in-law was saying or how much she knew but the words she was using combined with her own dirty fantasies were making her head swim. She could feel her pussy clenching as they continued this weird conversation.

"Good girl." Sonali nodded approvingly "I just wish Vikas wasn't so shy about taking advantage of Shriya. On the ship also I had to force him to let her massage him. He works so hard and gets stress, both physical and mental. Bahu is well-qualified, he should simply use her. There's nothing wrong in it."

"Don't worry, mom." Kajal said "I will arrange it. You are absolutely right. He should use Bhabhi whenever he needs. But don't worry, I will take charge of it. I will arrange these sessions regularly, have Bhabhi come over and do him may be once a month or twice a month. Bhabhi, would you be able to come and stay overnight some time? He can take time easier in evening than weekends."

"Kajal, I will do whatever he needs." Shriya said "He is an absolute angel. I will come and stay overnight once a week if you want. Just tell me."

"That's nice, Bhabhi." Kajal hugged Shriya "We have a guest room where you can sleep. And maybe massage him there too."

"Yes, that would be fine." Shriya said. In her head she was already wondering if the guest room would have enough privacy that Vikas could fuck her. She was sure she could suck his dick without making much noise.

"I mean, you could sleep in the master bedroom with me also, I don't mind." Kajal said "The guest bedroom doesn't have AC."

Before Shriya could reply Sonali said "You and Kajal are like sisters. Why would you be shy with her? And Vikas is your nandoi, you have given him massage. Why are you so shy with him?"

"I am not, mummy ji," Shriya protested "Kajal is really my sister, and I love Vikas dearly. I am happy to serve in any way I can. Nothing would give me more pleasure than keeping my nandoi happy."

Sonali cupped Shriya's cheek and smiled "Good girl."

Chapter 17 – Shriya Joins the Gym

"Shriya, shall we go take care of your gym thing today?" Vikas said to Shriya in the morning.

"Umm…Hemant.." Shriya looked at her husband "can you go to office yourself? I will go with Vikas to the gym."

"Can't you go another day?" Hemant said irritated.

"Well, I can go any day, but Vikas may not have time." Shriya said, also irritated by her husband's selfish attitude.

"Ok, Ok. I will go to the office from here. You go do your gym." Hemant said.

Shriya shook her head and said to Vikas "Yes, I can go with you. And thank you."

"No problem." Vikas turned to Kajal who was placing breakfast on the table "Kaju, I will go to this gym with Shriya, and go to the office from there."

"Jee, patidev." Kajal replied "I will go to our home and take care of things then."

"Okay. I will see you there in the evening, baby."

In the car, Shriya said "Actually, you didn't need to come. I could have gone alone. I feel bad having you waste your office time for me."

"Nonsense. Why should you go alone? Office is office but family is more important."

"You always put family first that's so nice."

"Actually, Shriya, I wanted to check out the gym, too. If it's good, then Rhea and Guddu can also join."

"Ok. But if it's not good?"

"Then you won't join either. We will find something better for you."

"Vikas, I love that you always take care of everybody." Shriya put her hand on his forearm.

Glancing at her hand on his forearm, Vikas looked at her "Hey, don't start that again now." He teased her.

"I know you said you won't be able to do me here, but I am going to get all slim and sexy after doing gym until you look at me and say 'I have to have that piece under me.'" Shriya smiled.

"Uff! What a cunning plan!" Vikas grinned.

They both laughed.

The gym was good. Vikas liked it and talked to the manager about getting a discount for 3 memberships. The manager was a beautiful woman called Malaika Arora who was very slim and fit herself. She was all about "building relationships".

"Shriya was telling me that you run an ad agency?" She asked Vikas.

"Yes." Vikas said.

"Well, we have many fit and toned girls in our gym. How about you give some of them a chance in your modelling and we give you a nice discount?" She said half-jokingly.

"If they are as hot and full of sex-appeal as you are then it's a deal." Vikas smiled letting his eyes roam boldly over her slender figure in her tight dress that hugged every well-toned curve of her body "Actually, I might have a project that would suit you perfectly. Have you been on camera before?"

"You are a charmer, Mr. Malhotra. I should be very careful around you." Malaika laughed and looked at Shriya "He is a charmer, isn't he?"

Shriya said "Oh, you have no idea."

They got 3 annual memberships for less than the price of two. Shriya was very excited as they left. Vikas dropped her home.

Chapter 18 – Shriya Thanks Vikas

At her place, Shriya said "You have to come in, even if for a minute. It looks really bad if I am just coming home in a stranger's car who drops me and goes."

Vikas nodded "Alright."

Shriya led him directly to the bedroom. She took off her clothes and came into his arms.

Pressing her naked, hot body against him, she squeezed until her soft, firm breasts were pressing on his chest through the clothes. She turned her face up and Vikas kissed her. She parted her lips for Vikas' tongue and within seconds it was like the hotel room in Thailand. She was grinding her pussy on his crotch and knew that he was not going to leave here without fucking her.

The kiss was hot and loaded with sexual tension. Shriya massaged Vikas' tongue with her own, giving him full access to her mouth. Her hand was massaging the back of his head. She opened her mouth, pressed her lips harder on his lips and swallowed his saliva as they carried with the lustful hot, passionate kiss.

His hands moved down, cupping her bare ass. She moaned into his mouth as she squeezed, kneading her firm ass cheeks in his strong fingers. She moved her body expertly, pressing her ass into his hands while grinding her pussy on his hard dick that she could feel outlined in his pants.

"It's not Thailand," Shriya panted as they broke the long kiss for want of breath "it's you. You are the one who brings out the whore in me. Now, take your whore and show me that your cock still owns me."

He did.

Vikas took only a minute to take off his clothes. Then he picked Shriya up and dumped her on the bed. She opened her arms and legs.

Vikas mounted her and in two seconds flat his cock was buried deep inside her, lodged tight in her cunt like a live missile.

"Ah, Vikas!" she moaned at the forceful penetration.

Her arms went around his naked body and she clung to him tightly. He started moving his hips, fucking her wet, tight pussy with in and out strokes. Shriya moaned and moved her hips with him, helping him penetrate her deeper. She knew it would hurt more in a second when he invaded her fully but she had already missed his cock in the last few days and was looking forward to him claiming her roughly.

"Mumma!" She cried out as Vikas used the hard thrust that jammed his cock fully deep into her cunt, his cockhead slamming into her cervix.

She took deep breaths to try and adjust to his cock and bear up the hot pain that had spread out from her pussy towards her extremities like a high-voltage current. Shriya had been so hungry for fucking recently that she had got her husband to fuck her one night. But after being masterfully demolished and conquered by Vikas in Thailand, the quick and boring session with her husband had left her more frustrated than satisfied.

Now that she was under Vikas again and his huge cock was ripping her apart, Shriya's body was responding with incredible arousal. She was already feeling a big orgasm building up in her pussy like dark clouds on the horizons cooking up a big and scary storm.

"Aah!" A long, deep scream escaped her lips as Shriya came hard, her body jerking under Vikas so hard that she lifted her ass off the bed.

He continued his long, deep strokes into her and sucked her neck as he fucked her expertly. Shriya squirmed under him and fucked herself furiously on his throbbing cock. When he came in her, she felt the heat spreading from her centre and let out another long moan. Her pussy responded to his hot cum burning through her body with several hot, erotic aftershocks that made her pussy clench.

She clung to his naked body as he fucked her with slow, long strokes, his thick cock making wet, squishing sounds as it drilled her soppy, wet cunt. Shriya took his head in her hands and kissed him hard.

"Vikas, you have spoiled me for all other men." She said looking into his eyes "No other man can satisfy me now and I can never say no to your cock."

"How many other men do you want to fuck?" Vikas smiled.

Shriya laughed "Please, feed your whore."

A soft sigh left her lips as he pulled out of her slowly. He lay down on his back and Shriya quickly got on her knees. She smiled and started to lick his cock. She let him see how much she enjoyed eating his cum. He stroked her head as she ran her tongue slowly along his shaft and licked up his creamy cum. She let it slide over her tongue before swallowing it.

"Would you like something to drink?" She asked him a few minutes later when they were both dressed.

"Just a glass of water. I am dehydrated for some reason." He grinned.

She smiled and got him a glass of water.

"Vikas," Shriya said standing close to him "I said it before and I am telling you again. It's all yours. Take me when you want. I will come wherever you call me. Think of me as your property."

He nodded and leaned in. "You are a delicious dish," he kissed her neck "once a man has tasted you…mmm now you are on my menu."

She laughed "You make me feel so hot and dirty with a simple sentence."

Chapter 19 - Parineeti Picks Up a Piece

"I am sorry, we don't have anything for you right now. But we have your headshots, we will call you if anything comes up."

Parineeti was just leaving a cheque at the Kansal Talent Agency when she saw the casting manager escort out a girl with the standard line used to reject models and actors.

She looked over the girl. In Pari's opinion she was very sexy. Her features were a little anglo-Indian rather than traditional Indian but she was definitely hot and had a great body.

The outfit she was wearing was very simple but very sexy. She was wearing a long white silk shirt which was quite translucent. It showed her white demi-cup bra inside that showed her beautiful breasts in a nice cleavage. She had buttoned only the middle four buttons and the shirt covered up to her thighs but was open to show her blue denim shorts. Her long, well-toned legs were fully bare. On her feet she was wearing 7" high stilettos that had multiple thin straps going over her instep but not covering her toes.

"Hi, excuse me!" Parineeti caught up with the rejected model as she left the agency.

"Oh, hi, are you talking to me?" The girl turned but didn't stop.

"Yes, what's your name?" Parineeti fell in step with her.

"Nargis Fakhri." The girl said "Yours?"

"Parineeti Chopra." Parineeti said "Did you just get rejected at Kansal's?"

"Yes." Nargis made a face "You too?"

"No, I am not a model." Parineeti said "But I want to talk to you, Maybe I can help you. Will you come to my office? It's not far."

"You have an office?" Nargis said.

"Well, it's not my office, I work there."

"Sure. So, you are not a model?"

"No, I am a secretary." Parineeti said.

"Ok. Where is your office?"

"Just 5 more minutes walk, see that corner, just there."

"Well, I have time, why not? Let's go." Nargis said.

Parineeti led her back to VisCom. As she started to walk to the door, Nargis stopped "You work here? You work at VisCom? Why didn't you say so?"

A smile lit up Parineeti's face "You know it?"

"Of course, I know it. All the struggling models know it. This is a great agency. They make so many projects every year, and they use new models a lot. But they don't take models directly, that's why I was trying at Kansal's. I have heard Rohit Kansal is a friend of the VisCom CEO and they take models only from Kansal's."

"That's all true." Parineeti said "But they don't take models directly doesn't mean they can't. There are exceptions."

"Wow, I can't believe you brought me to VisCom." Nargis said and followed Parineeti in.

"So, what do you do here?" Nargis asked as she got in the lift with Parineeti.

"I am the CEO's personal." Parineeti said with a touch of pride.

"Shut the front door!" Nargis exclaimed.

Parineeti's smile got wider. She led Nargis to her office and loved how awestruck Nargis was.

Once they were settled in her office, Parineeti faced the other girl and asked "So, do you really want to join VisCom as a model?"

"Yes! Very much so." Nargis said.

"What are you ready to do for it?"

"Everything!" Nargis replied without hesitation.

"You know how models are auditioned, don't you?" Parineeti boldly looked into her eyes.

"Of course." Nargis said carelessly "I wouldn't be trying to become a model if I weren't ready to do casting couch. That would be just stupid."

"Good. Normally, my boss doesn't get into recruitment." Parineeti said "But I think you are very hot and he would be interested."

"You think so?" Nargis moved to the edge of her seat "What do I need to do?"

"Can you wait for a while?" Parineeti asked "He is not here yet. He is coming in late today."

"How long do I need to wait?" Nargis said then added "It doesn't matter. I will wait as long as it takes."

"It won't be too long, maybe a couple of hours max." Parineeti assured her.

"That's no problem." Nargis said.

"Good, now let's fix your clothes. You won't get selected like this."

"Oh!" Nargis pouted "What should I change?"

"Well, my boss doesn't like shorts."

"But…I don't have any skirts right now. I can go get one." Nargis said.

Parineeti shook her head "You don't need it. Just take the shorts off. Are you wearing panties?"

"Yes, a thong."

"Take it off."

"But…then…I will be…

"Just button one more button at the bottom and open this button…"

She had Nargis take off her shorts and bra then button the shirt in a way that it was creating a nice deep cleavage on top. At the bottom it was showing her bare pussy through the two parts of the shirt when she walked.

"I feel so indecent." Nargis said.

Parineeti said "If boss likes you, he will fuck you right away. So, don't dress for audition, dress to be fucked."

"And if he doesn't like me?" Nargis asked.

"Then bad luck." Parineeti shrugged "I can't do any more. You will only get one chance to make an impression."

"Hmm. You are right. He needs to see that I am ready and willing." Nargis said "This is a big, big chance for me. I don't want to blow this."

"Exactly. Loosen your hair, put it in a ponytail. Boss likes to pull hair when he's fucking a girl."

"I am so glad you are helping me." Nargis started taking the hairclips out of her hair "Being boss' personal you know everything he likes."

"Of course. I have been working under him for a long time." Parineeti smiled proudly.

Chapter 20 – A Quick Tryst With Sonali

Vikas drove to Sonali's.

"Hello Sasu maa," he said loudly as Sonali opened the door "I left my briefcase here."

Sonali let him in and closed the door.

"Nobody's home." She told him with a sultry smile.

Two minutes later, their naked bodies were intertwined on her bed with Vikas' hard cock buried fully deep in her cunt.

"Mmmm, Damad ji," Sonali moaned in his ear "I missed you so much. Please fuck me at least once a week. I get so hungry for your cock."

"We will need to find a way, Sasu maa." Vikas rolled his hips fucked his mother-in-law slowly, keeping his massive cock stuffed inside her and grinding his cockhead in her cervix. She moaned with the incredibly deep strokes and pushed her hips forward to fuck herself on his throbbing beast.

"Oh god. Please, please, let me cum, Damad ji." Sonali begged as her body got so hot she could not contain it any more.

"Not until you tell me who you belong to, Sonali." Vikas sucked her neck and kept fucking her with the same slow strokes, keeping her body at the boiling point but not letting her go over.

"Aaaah! You own me, Sir. I belong to you." Sonali's whispers were urgent and hungry "You own my heart, body and soul. I am your bitch, my owner, your personal whore…ah, please, please, my owner.."

"You may cum, my whore" Vikas rolled her over and got on top of her. He started to pound her into the bed with long, forceful thrusts that pushed his cockhead almost into her womb. Sonali yelped and screamed with each thrust.

"Oh maaa!" She screamed as her body exploded in a wonderful orgasm, overloading her senses with pleasure. She surrendered herself in her son-in-law's arms and rode her orgasm like a wild horse.

Vikas continued to fuck her hard and deep until his cock exploded in her cunt and started to flood her womb with his seed.

"Mmmmm, thank you for giving me your seed, Damad ji" Sonali whispered in his ear "I am so grateful for you taking me in your possession."

He kissed her lips "You are welcome, my property."

It was quite natural by now for Sonali to lick her son-in-law's cock clean and eat his cum. She looked up at him as she knelt between his legs and sucked her cum-soaked cock.

After licking his cock and balls clean, Sonali lay down next to him and put her hand on his bare chest.

"Your cum tastes wonderfully delicious, by the way." She told him.

"That's what Kajal says as well."

"My girl has good taste." Sonali smiled "Thank you for taking care of my daughter, Damad ji. I could not have found a better husband for her if I had searched the whole world."

Vikas smiled "Well, you know how much I love her."

"Yes. And do you know that Rhea is getting more obsessed you with every day?" Sonali said.

"I have noticed some signs." He nodded "You need to explain to her, make her understand."

"How can I blame her for having good taste in men, dear?"

"You know what I mean. She's my sister-in-law."

"And I am your mother-in-law." Sonali reminded him "And I have the taste of your cum on my tongue right now."

"It's not the same. She's young and innocent. And unmarried. You will need to think about her marriage also."

"She's young but not stupid. I can see she's falling in love with you and to be honest, I can't blame her."

Vikas started to object "Sasu Maa…"

"Listen, Damad ji, suppose I explain to her and she understands me. Then what?"

"Then, I suppose she will find a boyfriend for her in her own age group, or you can find her a husband."

"I am not finding her a husband until she has her career started well. I want her to reach the stars not become a housewife like my Amisha. She had so much promise."

"Well, then let her enjoy her life and work on her career for a while."

"If I let her enjoy her that means she will find a boyfriend. She is very attractive and men flock to her like iron filings to a magnet."

"Nothing wrong with that."

"Do you think her boyfriend will fuck her?" Sonali asked.

"I am sure he will. That's part of a relationship."

"Yes, it is. And I am far from a prude. But will he be good at it? More importantly, will he be a good man?"

"We hope so."

"Yes, you can hope, Damad ji, because you don't know how few good men you find in the world. I know because I have watched Kajal make bad decisions one after the other. And Amisha, don't get me started on that."

"But…"

"Please don't say that you are a bad man because you fuck a few girls," Sonali caressed his cheek "or because you own your mother-in-law. You have proven on every step that you are a decent man and my daughter is lucky to have found you."

"Thank you, Sasu maa, but we were talking about Rhea's boyfriend."

"Yes, and in a good scenario I can expect that they will have a good relationship for a couple of years, she will have disappointing sex for most of that time until he gets bored then they will separate."

"That's the good scenario?" Vikas raised his eyebrow.

"It is. And the bad ones are so bad it doesn't bear thinking about."

"Why disappointing sex though?" Vikas asked.

"Because most good men are not good in bed. Most men good in sex are man whores who fuck around a lot." Sonali said in a matter-of-fact tone "I have seen the world from a woman's perspective, Damad ji, finding a man who is good and also good in bed is like finding a unicorn covered in gold."

"Hmmmm. I think you are being pessimistic but I can't say you are too wrong."

"Instead, if she is in love with a man I already know is a good, decent man, and she is enjoying good sex with him, I won't worry. I will know my daughter is safe and enjoying her life. After a few years, I can get her married, once I find a good man who will take care of her.”

“What are you asking me to do, Sasu maa?”

“I am not asking you to do anything, my handsome son-in-law.” She turned her face to him and kissed his lips “I am just saying don’t treat her like an untouchable just because she is your sister-in-law. She adores you. Let the poor girl have some love in return.”

“You are blowing my mind right now.”

“Let me blow something else then.” Sonali said with a cheeky smile and got on to her knees.

For the next twenty minutes she sucked her son-in-law’s cock. Kajal was young and eager to learn how to suck cock well but Sonali was already an expert. She licked Vikas’ cock slowly, first up the side, then she swirled her tongue around his cockhead like licking the top of an ice cream cone.

It took Vikas only a couple of minutes to get rock hard. Sonali closed her mouth around his cockhead and slowly pushed her head down. Her pace was so slow that Vikas could feel the heat gradually moving down towards the base of his shaft. When his bulbous cockhead hit the back of her throat, Sonali paused, looked up into his eyes and pushed hard once. The hard cockhead popped into her throat.

“Aaah!” A long moan escaped Vikas’ lips.

Sonali maintained eye contact as she sucked his cock deep, fucking it with her mouth and throat. She slowly increased her place until she could feel him bucking his hips and fucking her throat. Then she bobbed her head up and down, feeling him throb in her throat. She pulled back just as he was about to cum and fucked his cockhead with only her mouth. When his cock erupted in her mouth, she closed her lips tight and swallowed it all. Then she sucked him clean.

Chapter 21 – Gym Memberships

 "Wow!" Rhea exclaimed "Jiju got us gym memberships! We didn't have to ask and he already did it! He's awesome!"

Guddu agreed "He is great. I could not dream of joining that gym. It's so expensive, but Vikas jiju is always thinking of us."

Sonali sat down on the sofa with her book "Vikas had promised to help Shriya with her gym membership. He went with her and Shriya was saying he got you all a good discount by getting 3 memberships at the same time."

"That's so cool! I will go to the gym everyday. And mom, I will keep my promise to jiju. I will not drink at all any more." Guddu said.

"Good boy. I am happy he's having a good influence on you. Vikas himself drinks, but he's always in control and never irresponsible."

"Speaking of promises," Rhea chipped in "jiju is going to take me out clubbing with him in my new dress that he bought me before the wedding. You will let me go, na?"

"Of course!" Sonali said "Why would I stop you from going with Vikas? You will always be safe with him."

"Yay! Thanks, mom." Rhea cheered "I will remind him of his promise when he comes over. Will he come tonight, mumma?"

Chapter 22 – Vikas Auditions a Model

"Good afternoon, Sir." Parineeti said as Vikas came to office.

Vikas smiled "Good afternoon, darling."

Things had been a little awkward in office since yesterday when she had declared her love for Vikas and he had declined it. But Parineeti was determined not to let it ruin her relationship with Vikas. She had decided that she would continue with the relationship as it was before and hope that in time Vikas will change his mind. She was feeling things would have gone there in their natural progression but she had ruined it by being too eager and jumping the gun.

She followed Vikas into his office and as soon as he had sat down in his chair, she slipped into his lap. She boldly put her arms around his neck and kissed him on the lips with her soft lips parted. Vikas didn't seem to mind. He squeezed her in his arms and sucked her lips. His tongue pushed into her mouth with the same ease as before and they shared a kiss that was hotter than before, if anything.

Parineeti was wearing a tight white minidress that had no back. She had deliberately left her bra and panties off. Her soft full breasts pressed hard on his chest and she could feel the electricity flowing into her body. Her ass was resting right on his rod and his growing hardness was clearly felt on her ass. This gave Parineeti hope that he liked her and hopefully, some day he will come over his gentlemanly objections to claim her as his.

When they broke the kiss, Parineeti said breathlessly "Thank you, Sir. Now my day starts."

Vikas smiled "My pleasure."

"I need to ask you something, Sir." Parineeti said and when he nodded she continued "We only hire models from Rohit sir's agency. But if you found that a model was worthy would you make an exception?"

"Of course, darling. We are not bound by that system, and we are going to change that anyway. But yes, we can hire a model directly for a project if we want."

"Great. Can I show you something? Something that I think you would like?"

"Something? I thought you were talking about a model."

"I am." Parineeti nodded "She is such a beautiful piece, Sir."

"Piece, huh?" Vikas grinned.

She bit her lip and nodded "Very nice piece."

"Ok."

"Please check her out, and if you like her, please give her a good audition."

"What's a good audition?" Vikas said.

"One that she would remember tomorrow when she can't walk." Parineeti bit her lip again.

"Hmmm, that kind of audition." Vikas grinned.

"Yes, Sir. She is all ready, just waiting for you."

"Alright, let's see what this hot piece is like."

"I have go to get her, Sir." She got off his lap "I will be right back."

Parineeti had stashed Nargis in Secretary Pool on the other side of the floor. Now she went and told her to come with her.

"You know what, lose the ponytail." Parineeti said as they were walking "Leave it loose."

"Ok." Nargis quickly undid her ponytail and let her hair flow down her shoulders. It was not very long, just past her shoulders. But Parineeti was right, it framed her face beautifully.

Parineeti took her hand and entered Vikas' private office.

"Sir, please meet Miss Nargis Fakhri." Parineeti said "Nargis, meet boss."

Nargis was nervous. She felt like this one meeting was more important than all her struggles so far.

"Hello Sir. I am Nargis Fakhri." She repeated unnecessarily.

"Nice to meet you, Nargis." Vikas stood up "Vikas Malhotra."

From behind Nargis, Parineeti mouthed "Isn't she hot!"

She did indeed look a thousand times hotter than how Parineeti had found her. Her long, silk shirt was the only thing she was wearing now. Her sleeves were opened and pushed up. Her collar was pushed open so wide that part of her shoulders was visible. This way a lot more of her chest was bared. The first button that was done up was just below her tits and the cleavage was very deep and bold. Two more buttons were closed below that. Parineeti had not allowed her to close the button just over her pussy and the result was that her smoothly shaved pussy was peeking slightly from between the two sides of the shirt even as she stood there being inspected by Vikas.

Her long legs were a beautiful sight in all their toned, shapely nudity. Her feet were encased in grey stilettos with 8" high pointed heels. The high heels pushed her ass up and back in a sexy, inviting manner. Courtesy of Parineeti, Nargis was now wearing red lipstick which was Vikas' favourite shade.

Parineeti said "Should I hold your calls, Sir?"

Vikas smiled "Yes, please hold my calls for an hour. Let me talk to Nargis in peace."

"Yes, Sir." Parineeti exited quickly, closing the door behind her.

"Come, Nargis, let's talk." Instead of telling Nargis to sit, he called her over to him.

Nargis walked around his desk and came close to him.

"So, you are a model?" Vikas said and gently brushed her hair from her cheek.

Her head moved in a nod, then she added "I am trying to be, Sir." She was finding it intimidating to be talking to the CEO of a big agency who could make her career with one word from his mouth. Also, the other casting directors and agents that Nargis had met were usually middle-aged men with a paunch and dressed like used-car salesmen. She was finding Vikas' looks very distracting and nerve-wrecking.

"Well, you are definitely pretty," He said as he kept her close, by simply letting his hand linger at her hip. Nargis could feel the warm of his hand through her thin shirt "and you have good sex appeal."

"Thank you, Sir." Nargis was liking how this was going. The way he was treating her showed that he liked or was at least interested.

"Let's see if you can pose." He said and tapped his desk "Keep your back to the desk and pose against it."

Nargis perched her ass on the edge of the desk and stood with left leg straight. She bent her right knee.

"Hmmm, not bad." Vikas stepped closer and let his hand caress slowly along her left thigh "This leg is good, but this one," he ran his hand along the inside of her right thigh "keep the knee bent but bring it forward. Don't push the foot back, bring the knee forward."

Wherever he touched, Nargis could feel a hot current flowing into her body. She took his direction and adjusted her pose.

"Good girl." He nodded "Now, we don't have a camera but let's suppose I took a picture then…"

"You could use your mobile phone, Sir." Nargis suggested. She liked it when he smiled and said "Smart girl. Yes, I can."

He picked up his phone and took a picture "Good. Now change."

Nargis moved and cross her ankles in front of her. She put one hand on the desk, holding the edge. Vikas nodded, then stepped closer.

"Good, but for this one, chin up," he tilted her chin up with his fingers "and chest pushed forward." Nargis pushed her chest forward.

Vikas let his hand gently caress her firm, full breasts through the thin shirt "They are very nice."

"Thank you, Sir." Nargis said.

"I like that you came ready to…pose." Vikas said, letting his fingers follow the curve of her breasts through the thin fabric.

"Always ready for whatever the boss wants, Sir." Nargis said with a sweet smile.

Vikas reached inside her pulled out one breast. He adjusted the shirt so it went around the outside curve of her breast.

"Hold the shirt here," he put Nargis' hand on the shirt, just below her breast "pretend like you are trying to close your shirt, but don't actually close it."

Nargis posed as he said and Vikas took a picture. When he moved closer to her again, Nargis asked "Am I doing ok, Sir?"

"You are doing very well, darling." Vikas fondled her soft, warm breast then leaned down and touched his tongue on her erect nipple.

Nargis moaned. She placed her hand behind his head and pressed his mouth more on her breast. Vikas took more of her fleshy breast in his mouth, his tongue teasing her nipple.

"God, that feels so good, Sir!" Nargis caressed his neck with her warm hand.

Vikas lifted his head and kissed her lips softly, his hand fondling her breast, his thumb flicking the nipple slowly up and down. Nargis pushed forward as he pulled back and pressed her lips hard on his lips. Placing her hand behind his head, she kissed him passionately. She opened her mouth and licked between his lips. His fingers tightened on her warm, pliant breast as the kiss grew hotter and their tongues battled the lustful fight. Nargis pressed her lips again and again on his lips and locked them there to drink his saliva. Vikas teased her tongue with his and she moaned lustfully as she pressed herself into him.

"Mmmmm God!" Nargis moaned as they parted "What's the next pose, Sir?"

He reached down and opened all her shirt buttons, then parted the two sides of the shirt. Now all her beauty from her breasts down to her bare pussy was openly visible. Nargis gasped as he did it but didn't stop him.

"Now pose against that wall." He told her.

The wall was a half-wall that divided the two sides of Vikas' office – the desk area and the conference area. It started from the door side and went only half-way deep into the large room. Vikas wasn't sure it was really useful but it did provide privacy in case he wanted to have a meeting around the small table in the conference area and didn't want it to be seen by anyone entering the office. He had never used it for that reason so far though.

As Nargis stood with her back to the wall, she bent one knee and placed her high-heeled shoe on the wall behind her. Her shirt was open and showing everything but she posed boldly without a trace of self-consciousness. Vikas took photos, adjusted her pose and took photos again.

"Please, Sir," Nargis said, taking her shirt off and dropping it on the floor "please, take my audition."

Vikas put his phone down and walked up to her. She put her arms around his neck as soon as he was close enough and they kissed again, harder and hotter. Nargis parted her lips and Vikas pushed his tongue into her mouth. He ravaged her luscious, warm lips roughly with his hot lips. Nargis surrendered to his hard, rough kiss and pressed her body into him until her full, firm tits were squashed on his chest.

Reaching down, Vikas unzipped his pants and took his cock out. Nargis continued to kiss him but quickly stepped out on her high heels to open her legs wide. She whimpered into his mouth as she felt his thick, swollen cockhead push into her tight cunt. Vikas pushed again and jammed more than half of his long, hard cock into her tight, wet cunt.

"Ah!" Nargis screamed loudly and let the kiss break as the pain of his penetration shook her body.

Vikas kept her pinned back against the wall as he kissed her neck and started to move his hips, fucking her juicy, wet cunt in and out. Nargis held on to him and moved her hips, opening her legs wide to let him fuck her deep. She could feel his thick cock throbbing inside and his grinding movements inside her pussy were driving the temperature of her body into the scorching hot zone.

With a few smooth, forceful thrusts Vikas jammed his cock fully deep into Nargis' pussy and she yelped like a kicked puppy, her whole body pulsing with the sexual energy flowing through her. She kissed and sucked his neck, mumbling needy, dirty words in his ear.

"Yes, oh god yes!" She moaned "Fuck me like that, Sir. Hard! Just take me hard, Sir!"

Being a beautiful girl with a killer body, Nargis was used to being admired and appreciated. Most men were too intimidated to approach her and the ones who did…well, she was very choosy about picking dating partners. She loved sex and for her dating definitely meant sex, so she never said yes to anybody she didn't immediately want to fuck. She had been on a couple of casting couches but most casting agents and agency heads were past their prime and could hardly handle a young, strong beauty like her. While she had to spread her legs for them, she didn't really do it for pleasure, only for the sake of her career.

This, to her, was a rare opportunity, to meet a man who was a good-looking hunk but also powerful enough to give her career an atomic boost. Her body and mind were enjoying this encounter immensely. His big hard cock was like a dream come true for Nargis and she was riding it like it was her screen test. His cock was grinding on her gspot and Nargis was moaning with desire, not even caring if the office was soundproof or not.

Vikas changed his angle of entry and Nargis screamed as his cock crushed her clit when it entered her from a different angle. Another stroke and another scream as she tried to hold on, closing her arms tightly around his body. On the third stroke her pussy exploded and she moaned in a fast-paced rhythm as she came all over his cock. The orgasm was flooding her whole body with such delicious sensations that Nargis was not able to control the noises that were coming out of her mouth. She rode his thick, throbbing cock like a hungry little whore, moving her ass up and down taking him as deep as she possibly could.

"God, that was mind-blowing, Sir." She breathed in his ear "Please don't stop fucking me. I will audition whenever you want."

Slipping his dick out of her wet cunt, Vikas took her hair and bent her over his desk. Nargis quickly spread her legs open and pushed her ass back. In those high heels, with not a stitch of clothing on her body, she looked stunning hot. Vikas jammed his cock deep into her cunt from behind without any preamble. Nargis screamed as her body rocked forward with his hard thrust, then she started to push back to help him fuck her deep as he wanted.

Going down to her forearms on the glass desktop, Nargis held on with both hands flat on the glass and pushed back, following his rhythm as he fucked her in and out. His hand was still holding her hair and Nargis was glad Parineeti had made her loosen her hair. She was loving how he was banging her hard and without mercy. Her body was reaching towards another climax like a racing car and Nargis was getting ready for the explosion that was coming. Vikas was keeping her bent over in place as he drilled her like a beast, using her beautiful, young body like she was meant to be his fucktoy.

"Ah, god!" Nargis cried out as her pussy erupted again. Vikas reached down and grabbed her tits in both hands. As he kneaded her soft, fleshy mounds, Nargis could feel her orgasm spiking and her body going into overdrive. She tried to keep pushing back but her knees were buckling and she was losing control on her body. She lowered her head to the desk and let her forehead draw sweaty lines on the glass as Vikas continued to pound her cunt, rocking her body back and forth with his powerful strokes.

His hands crushed her soft tits, making Nargis whimper helplessly. She was feeling overwhelmed by the desire and passion she was experiencing for the first time in her young life. Her brain was flooded with the sex chemicals and she was falling in love with Vikas even as he was fucking her on his office desk. In her mind, she had already decided this was the luckiest day of her life and she was never going to give up a chance to have his dick inside her.

Suddenly, she felt him increase his speed and her hands slipped on the glass with his thrusts. His cockhead was now driving into her cervix, making Nargis realise how deeply he was claiming her. That thought of being not just fucked but claimed by this dominant man she had just met, pushed Nargis over the edge and she came again amidst hot, wanton moans. His cock erupted inside her the next moment and Nargis screamed as the heat flooded her body. She could feel his hot cum flowing through her body and flooding her womb. It made her feel more vulnerable than ever, but at the same time she loved it so much that she could not stop moaning continuously.

Lowering her body even more, she rested her face on the glass as she tried to catch her breath. Vikas was still fucking her but with slower in and out strokes which Nargis found delicious and addictive. She never wanted him to take his dick out of her. She moaned in a soft, relaxed rhythm with his strokes, already surrendering herself completely to him. His pulsing shaft felt so nice inside her, Nargis squeezed it with her pussy muscles, loving how thick it was.

When he did let his cock slide of her pussy, he took a fresh grip on her hair and guided her down to the floor. Nargis had sucked cock before, it was something she loved. She hadn't sucked one that had just fucked her but she was willing to learn. Under his guidance, she started to lick his cock. She licked his cum and ate it, at first because he wanted it but then she started to like the taste and that made her lick it with more interest. He was stroking her head as she was licking his cock clean and to Nargis that felt wonderful. As she licked his shaft and teased his cockhead, pushing her tongue into his pee hole to get the drops of cum from there, it started to rise. Then she licked under it and licked his balls to get the cum that was smeared on them.

She smiled up at him as she took his cockhead in her mouth and pushed her head forward, taking his semi-hard shaft into her hot mouth. He cupped her face and smiled as he caressed her soft, smooth cheek.

Nargis would have liked to suck his dick longer then take him in her again, but Vikas pulled her up and had her sit on his lap. He had zipped up but she could still feel his rod through his trousers on her bare ass.

"That was amazing, Sir." Nargis said "Best audition of my life! When can I come for round two?"

Vikas smiled "There's no round two, darling."

"Awww." Nargis pouted.

"No, no, you are selected. We will use you as a model." Vikas told her.

"Wow, that's awesome, Sir. Thank you so much!" Nargis paused then asked "What if I want to come for round two? Just so you can test me thoroughly."

Vikas laughed "That we can see. Let me check something."

He made a call on his desk phone and turned on the speaker phone.

"Shweta Tiwari here, hello?"

Vikas said "Hi Shweta, Vikas speaking. Darling, what projects do we have going right now? Any print ads where you need models?"

"Thank God, you called, Sir." Shweta said "We need three pretty girls for a commercial that's due in two weeks and Kansal's have been dragging their feet. We need to find another agency, Sir."

"We will, sweetheart. But ok, I have one girl for you, and I will see if we can find two more. I will talk to Rohit also."

"Amazing! That's great, Sir." Shweta said.

"Okay, I will talk to you later, darling. Let's keep on top of this."

"Yes, Sir."

"Wow. I can be that girl?" Nargis asked.

"You are that girl, sweetheart." Vikas said "I will get Pari to take you to HR. They will tell you what paperwork you need. Get that done as soon as possible then either this week or next week, we'll put you in front of the camera."

"So awesome. Please do call me back to your office. Any time. You can fuck me any way you like."

"That sounds good." Vikas said "I will see you soon then."

He let Nargis put her shirt back on then called Parineeti in and told her to take Nargis to HR.

Chapter 23 – Parineeti Working Hard

"I can't thank you enough, Parineeti." Nargis said as she was putting on her shorts and bra back on "I was so down when I was leaving Kansal's and this has been the most amazing day of my life! All thanks to you."

Parineeti smiled "You are welcome."

"Listen, how can I get another date with the boss?" Nargis asked, following Parineeti out to the lift.

"He is married, dear." Parineeti said "He doesn't date."

"That's fine by me." Nargis said casually "By date I mean, just ending up on his desk like today. Oh my god, he is mind-blowing. I mean, you know already but for me it was the best of my life!"

Parineeti didn't comment on that but asked "Has he asked you to come again?"

"No, he hasn't, but I really, really want to." Nargis got in the lift and turned to face Parineeti "Please, can you do anything?"

"I will try." Parineeti nodded "I will see if I can put you on his calendar later this week."

"Thank you, I owe you big."

==

Parineeti left Nargis in HR and came back to Vikas's office.

"I did notice she was walking a bit funny after her audition." She smiled at Vikas.

"Pari, what's on the other side of that wall?" Vikas said pointing to the far wall of his office, on the other side of the conference area.

"Not sure, Sir. I think there are storerooms or maybe a small office or two. Why, Sir?"

"I am thinking I need an attached bathroom there. We will see if it's possible." Vikas said "Sometimes after a good audition a girl needs to fix herself up before going out. The ladies' room in the corridor is not a good option for that."

"Awww, you are thinking about your model sluts, so sweet."

Vikas chuckled "You look very hot when you talk dirty."

"Well, there's an email from the LA agency we have been talking to," Parineeti said "would you like to answer that now or are you too tired?"

"Tired from what?"

"From the…you know…audition."

"No, we just talked." Vikas fibbed "I don't get tired from talking. Let's look at the email."

"Okay, great." Parineeti walked around his desk and calmly planted her butt in his lap "Let me find it for you."

Her white skin tight dress had a deep cleavage and no back. The two noodle thin straps that went over her shoulders went straight down instead of crossing in the middle of her back. Parineeti had beautiful, full breasts and the dress was doing a great job of pushing them up for a lovely, mouth-watering cleavage.

"Sure." Vikas wrapped his arm around her midriff and kissed softly just below the base of her neck "Take your time."

"Mmmm, you are a horrible boss, do you know that?" She leaned back and kissed his cheek "Here is the email."

As Vikas started to read the email, Parineeti took his hand from her belly and placed it on her breast.

"What's that?" Vikas said.

"Nothing, just keep reading." She held his hand on her breast. In the deep cleavage half his hand was actually resting on her bare breast. He let it be there and fondled her breast slowly as he read the email.

"Click on the attachment." He said, leaving his hand on her breast, and his left hand on her leg.

Parineeti took the mouse and clicked on the attached file in the email. It was a project plan.

"Okay, so they have filled out half of it and want us to provide the rest of the information." Vikas said "Seems fair. If we do this deal they will need to know about the Indian market just as they have told us about their LA operations."

"Yes, Sir. Do you want to send a reply now or after we make the full plan?" Parineeti leaned back on his chest.

"Let's send a holding reply for now so they know we are working on the plan." Vikas said.

"Ok, I will type," Parineeti slipped her left strap off her shoulder and placed Vikas' hand on her naked breast "why don't you keep me motivated?"

"Really? I am your assistant now?" Vikas said, but he didn't take his hand off her breast.

"Yes, and you are doing very well," Parineeti leaned back again and kissed his jaw "I might give you a bonus."

She boldly rubbed her ass on his dick before she pulled the keyboard to her and started to type. Vikas contributed some words and told her to use certain phrases, but mostly he watched her type and slowly kneaded her hot, bare breast, feeling it soft and firm in his hand.

Parineeti moaned as he kissed her neck. She could feel hot currents flowing from her breast to her fingers, but she kept typing.

"Send?" She said finally.

"Send." Vikas said. Parineeti clicked the Send button.

"Anything else or should I go back to my office?" She asked.

"Let's make a list of all the people I need to talk to in order to get that information." Vikas said "Then arrange meetings with them as soon as possible."

"Ok." Parineeti turned her face up and kissed him on the lips. He responded easily by sucking her bottom lip into his mouth. It was not a long kiss but had the easy intimacy that Parineeti wanted to develop.

Then she turned to the computer again and started typing "First one will be Rohit Sir, I am guessing?" She said.

"Yes, I need to talk to him, anyway." Vikas said, still playing with Parineeti's warm, soft breast "He's been letting the ball drop lately."

Parineeti moaned as he squeezed her breast but she kept working. She kissed him again after the list was completed. Then she went back to her office to start making the calls for those meetings. She was soaking wet when she walked out of his office.

Chapter 24 – Vansh is Summoned by the CEO

Vansh was just picking up his bag to go home when the desk phone rang. It was Parineeti Chopra, the CEO wanted to see him. He said he would be right up.

He had been waiting for the boss' email reply since the moment he sent that email yesterday morning. Now he got the response in the way of a phone call and a summons to his office. It was either very good or horribly bad. He stopped at Parineeti's office. She was gorgeous and she dressed so sexy and bold that the whole office stared at her. He tried not to stare at her legs in her beautiful short dress as she walked up to him and led him to the door that said "Vikas Malhotra – Private."

"Sir, Vansh Chaudhary is here." She said as she opened the door.

"Thank you, darling. Bring him in."

Vansh entered with trembling legs and was thankful when the boss told him to sit down. Parineeti went back to her own office.

"So, you work in our IT department."

"Y…yes, Sir." Vansh said.

"Not for long." Vikas said in a strict tone and Vansh's throat dried even more "I need dedicated people who love what they are doing not someone who is riding in two boats."

Vansh didn't know where to start defending himself. He had shot himself in the foot with his own hand. Everything was in his email. He could not deny anything.

"It's not…Sorry, Sir…no, Sir…" He tried.

Suddenly Vikas smiled. "I will transfer you to Still Photography." He said.

"Really?" Vansh was flabbergasted. He did hope that his email would lead to something good but he didn't expect it to be this good and this easy.

"Did you take these pictures? Really?" Vikas asked.

"Yes, Sir. Every one of them."

"Come here, bring your chair around."

Vanshi pushed the chair around to Vikas' side of the desk and looked at the pictures with him.

"They are good. Very good." Vikas said "Not that there's not room for improvement, but you have talent."

A smile lit up Vansh's face "Thank you, Sir."

"Your email shows you have passion for it." Vikas continued "You did really risk your job for it."

"It was a risk worth taking, Sir." Vansh said.

Vikas nodded "I am a photographer myself, you know, or used to be." He looked at Vansh "And now I sit behind this desk and write emails."

The silence that followed was uncomfortable. Vansh didn't know how to handle this particular situation with his super-rich, super-powerful boss complaining to him about his life. He would have thought any man would love to exchange places with him.

"But you don't have to do that." Vikas said "When you have a passion for something, go for it with all you have got."

"Photography is my only passion, Sir." Vansh stated.

"Good. Give me a few days, we'll find a replacement for you in IT, you will do your knowledge transfer to them and you will be transferred to Still Photography."

"Yes, Sir. Please take your time, Sir."

"Actually, I will see if we can have you wrap up in IT and start ramping you up in Photo in parallel. Are you open to do some extra hours so your work doesn't suffer in IT, if I can manage that?"

"That would be great, Sir. I will stay as long as needed."

"Ok, leave it with me, I will see what I can do. I will try and move you into Photo within this month."

"Wow, that would be awesome, Sir." Vansh enthused "I can't tell you how grateful I am!

"No worries, mate. I am happy to help." Vikas said "Oh, before I forget, who's the model you have used," he pointed to the screen where one picture was still open "is she a professional?"

"Kind of, Sir. She is my girlfriend." Vansh felt guilty that he had forgotten to ask about her completely in his excitement for his own opportunity "She's trying to get into modelling."

"What's her name?"

"Hina Khan, Sir." Vansh tried to make up for his previous oversight "She is absolutely fantastic, Sir. Very good with her own make up, amazing fashion sense, and a great model, Sir. She just needs a break. She is working as a waitress right now but her passion is modelling."

Vikas nodded "She looks promising. Can you get her to come in and talk to me?"

"Oh, yes, Sir. Any time you want, Sir." Vansh was really excited now.

"Good. Let me see." Vikas pressed the intercom button "Pari, can you come in?"

A moment later Parineeti was peeking in the door "Yes, Sir?"

"Sweetheart, do I have time in the next couple of days to see a new model?"

Parineeti said "Tomorrow afternoon is open right now, Sir. I am waiting to hear from someone, or you have an hour on Friday afternoon."

Vikas looked at Vansh. "Tomorrow, Sir." Vansh said quickly "Tomorrow afternoon, Sir."

"Are you sure she can make it?" Vikas said.

"Yes, Sir. She will make it, Sir." Vansh said with confidence. He knew Hina would kill for an opportunity like this.

"Darling, make it tomorrow afternoon, put the name…Hina?" Vikas looked at Vansh, who nodded several times in succession "Hina Khan. Vansh will call you in the morning and confirm."

"I will confirm tonight, Sir." Vansh said eagerly.

"Yes, but office will be closed, my friend." Vikas reminded him gently.

"Oh, yes." Vansh laughed nervously "I will confirm in the morning, ma'am." He said to Parineeti.

Parineeti nodded.

"Thank you, Vansh." Vikas said "Have a nice evening. I will see you soon, buddy."

When Vansh left Vikas' office, he was walking on air.

Chapter 25 – Vikas Visits the Travel Desk

Parineeti said "Are you going to stay longer, Sir?"

"No, my darling, I am just about done, that was my last action item of the day." Vikas said "Can I give you a lift?"

"I would love that." Parineeti said.

"Would you mind if we stopped at travel desk for a minute?"

"Not at all."

They went down to the 11th floor.

Parineeti said "I will just say hello to Rani. I will be back in 5 minutes."

"Take your time. I will be about 15-20 myself."

"Great." Parineeti turned towards the HR department and Vikas walked into the Travel department.

"I knew I would find you working late again." He told the girl working there.

"Oh, hello Sir!" Neetu Chandra said excitedly as she saw him. She came out from behind her desk and hugged him "Welcome back."

She was an attractive girl with a slender body. She was wearing a tight, red dress that reached down to her knees and looked very sexy. It was thin enough that she could feel his hand caressing down her back. Neetu had had a crush on Vikas since the day he had interviewed her for the job, but he had not made a move on her and she had not had to bend over his desk to get the job. In her fantasies, she had had a hard drilling on his desk for the job many times, but in reality she was only able to see him when she made an excuse to go and visit him or if he needed any travel arrangements done.

It was only since the engagement party that she had started hugging him and she carried on doing that as he didn't object. This was the first time she was seeing him after his wedding and she found that her attraction for him had not diminished after his marriage. If anything, it had increased. He looked very dashing in his business suit and slight stubble.

He kept his arm around her waist and Neetu stayed close to him. There was nobody else in the department at his hour and Neetu decided to be a little bold.

"The last time I saw you was when I came to your office with the travel tickets for your honeymoon. This is the first time I am seeing you after the wedding. I didn't get to congratulate you properly," She looked into his eyes then lowered her eyes "didn't even get to kiss the groom."

"I can't turn the time back, sweetheart, but," He said "I am here."

Neetu took that as a signal and pressed her lips on his while pressing her whole body against him. His lips were hot and rough, Neetu could feel his breath on her face and her whole body was turning on very quickly. She pressed her firm tits into his chest as she sucked his lips. When his tongue touched her upper lip, she welcomed it eagerly by parting her lips and taking it in. She placed one hand behind his neck and rubbed slowly as she swallowed his tongue into her mouth. His hands on her smooth back were rubbing slowly up and down. His fingers were sending little jolts of electric charge into her body through the thin dress.

"Mmmm, wow!" Neetu panted as they broke the kiss "Why do you always have to be a good guy?"

"What do you mean?"

"If it were someone else, he would have grabbed my butt when my mouth was on his."

"Ah, I missed my opportunity." Vikas said.

"Well, I can't turn back the time," Neetu said and bit her lip "but I am here."

Vikas laughed and let his hand slide down to her butt. Instead of grabbing it, he spanked it "Naughty girl."

"Ow!" Neetu fake-moaned "Isn't that why you like me?"

"I do like naughty girls, that's true." This time Vikas let his hand stay on her ass and slowly kneaded her ass cheek. Neetu stayed close, fully willing and compliant.

He perched his ass on her desk and pulled her with him. Neetu happily stood between his legs, her body charged with desire as his legs touched her lightly on either side. His hand was resting on the small of her back. She wanted him to continued kneading her ass but he had stopped for now.

"Darling, I need to interfere in your department a little bit." He said, gently caressing her lower back.

"You can interfere as much as you want, Sir." Neetu said "The department is yours, alongwith everything in it." She tried to end the sentence seductively to give him an idea that she was offering herself without saying that in so many words.

"Good girl." His hand slid a little lower this and he rubbed her firm, shapely ass casually "I need to look into the models accommodation that we maintain in the city."

Neetu took a chance and placed her hand on his chest "You mean the hotel rooms we maintain in the city for models who come from out of the city?"

Vikas nodded, his hand was now resting squarely on Neetu's butt, squeezing her tight ass cheek lightly as he kept her close to him "Yes, exactly. We will be expanding our business very soon and I want to see what options we have for upscaling as well as upgrading those arrangements. Then we need to decide which option we go with."

"Sure, Sir." Neetu rubbed his chest slowly as she looked into his eyes "I can give you all of that. Do you have time now?"

"Oh no, sweetheart," this time he squeezed her ass cheek harder as he pulled her close and kissed her cheek "it's already late, you should go home. But may be tomorrow or something, you can give me a tour of the hotel and we can talk about it?"

"Whenever you want, Sir." Neetu leaned in just a little bit to let her soft, firm tits press on his chest "I am at your beck and call."

"Great. I will ask Pari to fix something up." He said, letting her come closer and still kneading her ass cheeks slowly.

"Why don't you ask her now?" Parineeti said, walking in.

"Speak of the devil…" Vikas kept his right hand on Neetu's ass and continued kneading and squeezing her ass cheeks as he opened his left arm.

Parineeti walked around "Hi Neetu!" and came in his embrace from his left.

"Hi Pari!" Neetu said. She stayed where she was, in Vikas' intimate embrace.

Vikas pulled Parineeti close until her soft body was pressing on his body from the side.

"What do you need, Sir?" Parineeti asked.

"Baby, I need some time to discuss our model accommodations with Neetu, and she will take me on a hotel tour, you will, won't you, darling?"

"Of course, Sir, whenever you want." Neetu nodded.

"What time will be good, so we can meet the hotel management as well?" Vikas asked.

"Late morning or early afternoon, Sir." Neetu said.

"Babe?" Vikas looked at Parineeti. His left hand was on her bare back which he was caressing slowly.

"Well, Mrs. Shetty's secretary has confirmed the meeting for tomorrow morning, so you'll probably be free by noon." Parineeti said boldly pressing her tits into his side, unlike Neetu, she was confident of her place with him "Neetu, could you meet Sir directly at the hotel? He will already be close by there."

"Of course." Neetu said.

"Maybe you could treat the poor girl to lunch, Sir?" Parineeti suggested "Look how thin she's become. Then you could keep her until afternoon, you don't have anything till 4PM."

"Sounds good to me." Vikas slapped Neetu's ass "What do you say?"

"It's perfect, Sir." Neetu smiled "Thank you, Pari."

Parineeti grinned "It's what I do."

"Alright. Fantastic. Let's go home now then." Vikas said.

"I will email the hotel now so the manager is available for us tomorrow, Sir." Neetu said.

"Okay." Vikas said. He leaned in and pulled Neetu close for a kiss. She didn't hesitate and parted her lips for a hot, wet kiss, letting his tongue play in her mouth. His hand was kneading her ass cheeks the whole time.

"Goodnight, darling." Vikas said as they parted "I will see you tomorrow for lunch."

"It's a date, Sir." Neetu smiled.

Parineeti started walking out with Vikas then doubled back as soon as he was out the door.

 "Short dress, much shorter than this," She told Neetu in a quick whisper "he likes bare back. No panties." She looked at her shoes "Nice shoes but he likes high heels, stilettos are his favourite. You got platforms?"

"No," Neetu shook her head "but my roommate is a total slut, she has many."

Parineeti nodded "Great. Good luck."

"Thanks, I owe you one." Neetu said.

Chapter 26 – Dropping Off Parineeti

"Where did you get stuck?" Vikas said "The lift is already here."

"Sorry, just had to tell Neetu to email me the hotel address, otherwise where would you go?"

"Ah, good thinking."

Parineeti knew she hadn't asked for that address, but there was time before noon next day to get it from Neetu.

In the car, they talked about general things. Then Parineeti asked him about the cruise.

"So, these waitresses, really hot?"

"Oh, very!" Vikas said "Each hotter than the last. The whole ship was after them."

"But they were easy for you?"

"Hmmm," Vikas thought about it "I would say yes. I didn't have to make any special effort. But I don't know if they were fucking anybody else."

"Yes, you know." Parineeti said knowingly "They were not fucking anybody else, because I can bet they fell in love with you as well."

They were stopped at a red light. Vikas reached over and brushed her hair from her cheek "Not everybody is as gullible as you."

Parineeti stuck her tongue out at him. He laughed.

When they got close to her parents' place, Vikas pulled over a block away.

"Drop you here?" He asked.

"No, it's not late today so you can drop me at the door." Parineeti said, but she put her hand on his as he started to change gear "But you should kiss me goodnight here."

He nodded and turned the engine off.

"Push your seat back." Parineeti said. Vikas pressed the button that pushed his seat back all the way. Parineeti climbed over the middle section and straddled him in his seat.

She sat on his thighs and pressed her lips down to his. His hands caressed her bare back in her backless dress as they kissed. The kiss was hot and loaded with sexual tension. Parineeti pushed her tongue into his mouth and they shared a very hot, passionate kiss. It became more of a make-out session than just a kiss. When they parted, they were both completely breathless.

"Wow, that's some goodnight kiss." Vikas said.

"You have meetings and things tomorrow, so I won't see you until the afternoon." Parineeti said "This was goodnight and also good morning for tomorrow."

"Always planning ahead like a good secretary." He patted her ass.

Chapter 27 – Hina Gets Good News

"No way!" Hina said "Are you kidding me? I will kill you if you are joking."

Vansh was loving this "No, I am not joking. He has called you to see him."

"He wants to see me?" Hina pointed to herself "Me? Vikas Malhotra wants to see me, Hina Khan?"

"Yes, yes, yes, he wants to see you." Vansh could not stop grinning. He was the hero of her life right now and it was the best feeling in the world.

"And as a model? Not because I am your girlfriend, bring her around some time kind of thing."

"Well, he knows you because you are my girlfriend, but he asked if you were a professional model."

"Then he invited me?"

"Yes."

"Tell me everything!" Hina jumped once more before sitting down on the sofa and facing him.

Vansh started telling the story that he had told her once already "I emailed him yesterday morning, all those photos that we had taken for your portfolio—"

"Our portfolios." Hina interrupted.

"Yes, those, and I wrote like how I wanted to be a photographer."

"Why didn't you tell me?"

"I wanted to see if he would reply first." Vansh said "I didn't want to get your hopes up. He is very busy. He runs an ad agency."

"Oh, I know. Believe me, I know." Hina said "I have tried several times to meet him, but, well, as you say, he's busy. So, then he called you?"

"Well, his secretary called me, just as I was about to leave for the day. And she asked if I could come up and meet him."

He told the story again and Hina listened to it all again with the same wide-eyed wonder as the first time.

"I can't believe it. Wow!" She gushed "This is amazing. Just Amazing!"

She kissed him hard but quick "Thank you. Thank you so much, baby. Thank you, thank you, thank you."

Vansh grinned again. He had already said "You are welcome." about 20 times already.

"What time is it? 4 O'clock, right?" She knew the answer already.

"Mhmm." Vansh nodded.

"Awesome. I will be there, of course."

"I can't take you I will be in the office." Vansh said "But I can go up with you, if you want."

"No, no, I can't fuck it up. I need to go like a professional model." Hina shook her head "Did he say what I should wear?"

Vansh made a face "Why would he say that? No, he didn't."

"Would have made it easy." Hina started for her wardrobe and started rummaging "Did he like any of my pictures more than the others? Did you notice?"

"Ummm, I can't say. He seemed to like all of them." Vansh said "Oh yes, he had one photo open on his screen all the time he was talking to me."

"Oh great." Hina stopped rummaging and came to stand in front of him "Which one?"

"It was one of the ones we took in your yellow dress."

"Yellow? I have 2 yellow dresses in that shoot."

"The one that has corrugated vertical lines down the front."

"Pleats, baby. They are pleats." Hina laughed. She went to her phone and found the pictures "This one?"

"Yes, but he had the other picture open in this dress, from the back."

"Oh yes, this has a low back. He likes bare back then?" Hina asked.

"Probably. His secretary was wearing a dress with no back."

"His personal secretary?"

"Yes." Vansh said.

"He probably fucks her, baby."

"I think so too, he calls her baby, darling, all the time."

"Normal. Most bosses fuck their personal secretaries. It's quite normal." Hina said casually "She probably dresses as he likes. Tell me more about her dress."

"Well, it was white, quite short, and no back."

"Ok, then this yellow dress should be fine." Hina said "Does he like panties?"

"Huh? I don't know. How would I know?"

"Think. Was his secretary wearing any?"

"Oh, no, she wasn't."

"You sure." Hina asked.

"Totally. She came in when I was sitting inside, and when she was standing in the door, the corridor light was behind her, her dress was thin…no, she wasn't wearing panties."

"Ok, no panties then. Thanks, baby."

"What? Why?" Vansh was shocked

"You don't understand how modelling works, honey." Hina said "This is my one and only chance to impress him. If he likes me, my life will be set."

"But without panties?" Vansh said "That dress is so short and see through."

"When are you moving to photography?" Hina cleverly changed the topic.

"He said within this month." Vansh said "It takes time. If he can even do it this month, it would be great."

"Will you be working with me or other models?"

"Oh no, I will probably be just cleaning lenses for a few months. I won't get a chance to do a shoot for at least 3-4 months, you can count on that."

"Really? Why?"

"Because there are other senior photographers already in the team. I will be the most junior and without qualifications or professional experience. I will need to learn."

"Oh, I see. But at least you are on the track now."

"Yes, absolutely. I am so excited!" Vansh said.

While Hina was still going on about dresses and shoes, Vansh suggested gently if they could have sex.

"Sorry, baby, but Ruhi will be home soon. Also, you have office tomorrow, and I have a morning shift, so I need to get everything ready tonight so I can come here, change and leave right away tomorrow afternoon. I can't tell you, I will be so happy when I can give my notice at the restaurant. Or when I don't have to live with Ruhi, or any roommate."

"You only need a few assignments, baby, then you will start getting work on your own as soon as people see what a great model you are."

"Exactly! That's why it's crucial that I make my impression so he gives me a break." Hina said "What kind of a guy is he?"

"Seems quite nice for someone so powerful." Vansh said "He just got married a month ago."

"Yes, you told me, baby. He's just back from his honeymoon."

"Right, right." Vansh said. "I don't know if he still fucks his secretary then."

"Oh, it doesn't matter for bosses, honey." Hina said "She is his personal secretary then she is his property. He could have ten wives and he would still fuck her. And she would spread for him any time he wanted."

"You really think so?" Vansh said.

"I know so, baby." Hina told him "Power is extremely important for everything. She is pretty, right, his secretary?"

"Oh yes, like a supermodel."

"Then that supermodel is his personal whore, I can give you in writing."

"Wow!"

Hina said "Tell me about her shoes."

Vansh was jolted by this sudden change in direction "Huh? Whose shoes?"

"The secretary. What's her name?"

"Parineeti Chopra."

"Okay, tell me what kind of shoes she was wearing." Hina asked "You did notice, right? Or you were just looking at her boobs?"

"Ummm…" Vansh closed his eyes "Yes, yes. I noticed. They were high heels, very high, like this…and they had pointed heels, and what do you call it, umm, platform."

"Damn, I don't have anything this high with platforms. I will ask Ruhi when she comes."

"But you won't be able to walk in them, baby."

"Why not?" Hina demanded "I am a model. High heels are normal for me."

"I think they were about 8" high."

"Yes, I can do that fine." Hina said "Wish I had money, then I could go out and buy some shoes and dresses. Now I have to make the best of what I have. At least I have a few backless dresses."

When Vansh left a little later, Hina was still sorting out her dress and shoes.

Chapter 28 – Kajal and Vikas Date Thailand Style

"Don't you get bored staying at home?" Vikas said.

"Patidev, I have thought about it many times already, you gave me the choice to work or not work, and both have their advantages but…ah…there is a way other than the two."

"Yes?" Vikas moved his hips which made Kajal moan again "You have a plan, I am guessing?"

"Mhmmm." She moved her up, riding slowly up and down on his lap. His cock was buried deep inside her and her hands were on his shoulders "I do."

"Want to share?" Vikas ran his hands slowly down her bare back and kept her slowly bouncing up and down on his lap.

They were both fully naked. He was sitting on the long straight part of the sofa with his knees slightly bent. Kajal was skewered deep on his cock with her knees on the sofa, on either side of him. She was riding him slowly up and down as they chatted. She had texted him earlier than she wanted to have a Thailand style date tonight. Their Thailand style date was like this. It started with direct sex and everything else followed afterwards.

"Rhea has shown interest in doing fashion business," Kajal shared her plan as she continued to ride her husband's long, thick shaft "I will use my work experience to help her set it up…mmmm…it will be family so won't have restrictions like a job, and it will give me something to do that I will enjoy and not get bored."

"Sounds like a great idea." Vikas squeezed her ass cheeks and pushed deeper into her cunt so his cockhead started to grind on her cervix with the incredibly deep penetration "But you were always my smart slut."

"Aaah!" Kajal kept her legs open so he could be as deep inside her as he wanted but already her body was getting hotter "Thank you, honey. It goes without saying that I will only do this if you allow me to, Sir."

"Of course, that's your call, baby!" He leaned in and kissed her neck while his cock throbbed inside her soaking wet cunt.

"Mmm, may I cum, baby? Please?" Kajal asked with her eyes closed and her pussy squeezed his cock as she tried to hold on before cumming.

"No, not yet, my love!" Vikas said as he kept fucking her slowly but very deep.

The first word itself set Kajal's pussy on fire. She needed to cum and even though she had acted smart by asking for permission a little sooner than she really needed, just his denial had fired up her body into overdrive and now she really needed to allow her pussy to explode around his cock.

"Please, Sir!" Kajal leaned in and kissed his neck, whispering her urgent pleas in his ear "Please my wonderful owner, my master, please let me cum! Allow your whore to cum on your cock, please Sir."

"Not yet, my little whore!" He whispered in her ear, but even as he denied her the orgasm, he didn't stop fucking her. His cock continued to drill her hot pulsing cunt in and out as he held her firm, shapely ass in his hands.

"Oh, God! Master! Please, I am your whore. Please let me cum. Please have mercy on your whore, Sir. Aaah, God. Sir!" Kajal's whole body was buzzing like every cell in her body was flooded with extra blood. She could feel the hot currents rising not just in her cunt but all over her body. She was afraid her whole body would explode in another millisecond. Yet, there was no question of cumming without her owner's permission and she cried but held on to hear that one word from his lips.

"Now! You may cum, whore! Cum for me." Vikas said in her ear and speeded up his strokes, fucking her faster and harder.

Kajal's body exploded on his command. She lost control of her body and collapsed in his arms at the same time being thankful that he continued fucking her deep and hard. His cock hitting her cervix felt like the centre of her universe. She soaked his cock with her cum as her pussy gushed around his throbbing beast.

Then she felt him explode inside her and her orgasm still going strong, intensified to an incredible magnitude. Kajal was breathless and hot. Her body was glistening with sweat. Tears were dripping out of her eyes and flowing down her cheeks. She held on to Vikas like he was her only support in a stormy sea. She moaned and screamed as she came again and her hips, having a mind of their own, rode his throbbing hard cock fast and deep.

"Oh God!" Kajal breathed out after a few minutes "You are so bad, my husband."

"Why do you love me?" Vikas challenged.

"Because you are so bad, my husband." Kajal pressed her lips on his and kissed him hard with a furious kiss that was love, sex, passion, desire and lust all rolled into one. He kissed her back and they continued sucking each other's lips until they were both completely breathless again.

"Mmmm god!" Kajal whispered "I love you, my Owner."

"I love you, my darling." He kissed her cheek.

For a few more minutes, Kajal enjoyed having his not-so-hard cock inside her and rolled her hips, loving the feeling of riding her husband's cock. Then, when he allowed her, she got off his lap, knelt between his legs and licked him clean.

This had become one of Kajal's favourite thing to do. Not only did she love the taste of his cum, she loved showing him how completely she belonged to him and how much she loved worshipping him with her tongue. She gently caressed his thighs as she licked his cum from his cock, then lowering her head, from his balls. There was a big mess on the leather seat of the sofa where they were sitting. Kajal cleaned everything and ate all his cum happily before she stopped.

"That's like a good bitch." He smiled and caressed her cheek.

"Your bitch, Sir." She reminded him.

"Of course, my bitch." He agreed with a smile "My prized possession."

They had opened a bottle and even managed to pour wine into glasses before Vikas had pulled her down on his lap and everything else had been forgotten. Now, they picked up their glasses and sipped the wine as they sat close.

"That reminds me," Kajal said "thank you for letting Rhea come close to you. Can you see how happy it makes her?"

"Of course. I had no doubt about that but I was just thinking about her future." Vikas told her.

"Don't worry about that, Patidev," Kajal rubbed his chest "being with you is only going to motivate her to do bigger and better things. May I ask you another favour if you don't mind?"

"What now, girl?"

"I know very well that you are not one of those bosses who fucks the models on casting couch." Kajal said "And you must meet a lot of hot, slutty girls."

"Agreed. The average of sluts is higher than normal given that it's show business. So?"

"So, you have to fuck them and please bring me the stories." Kajal said.

"Hey, I have a business to run." Vikas reminded her.

"Do your business, Sir." Kajal suggested "But pound at least one model a day?"

"Wow, Thailand has corrupted you, girl." Vikas accused.

"Sir, Thailand opened my eyes. I so loved having you claim those sluts. And I loved having you in me as you told me about it. It was like double the pleasure. Please, please promise me you will take these gorgeous sluts and make them your bitches."

Vikas shook his head in a helpless gesture "I will see what I can do."

"Thank you, my owner." Kajal leaned in and kissed his cheek "You will do great."

"We will see."

"Oh, and don't break Pari's heart, please." She warned.

"Huh? Where did that come from now?"

"Look, patidev, you know and I know that that girl is madly in love with you." Kajal used her no-nonsense tone for this "She is probably still hoping that you would claim her. Don't you go breaking her heart."

"Where do you get these ideas, woman?"

"You are trying to deflect and it won't work with me, Sir. Pari worships the ground you walk on. And if you only treat her as a secretary that would be a cruel joke on the poor girl."

"So, you suggest that I fuck her."

"No, that's for the model sluts." Kajal corrected him "Pari does everything for you with a devotion. And all she wants is to be your possession. You need to give her that."

"Hmm, just so I am up to speed with your crazy ideas, what exactly is it that you are asking me to do?"

"Dear husband, this time I am not asking you, I am telling you," She looked into his eyes and then pulled back "please take her in your possession like she has been craving for so long."

"You have met her a couple of times and decided all this?" Vikas asked.

"I knew it when I met her the first time. Only men can be so blind that they don't see it. But you are not that kind of man. You know this. You know as well as I do how much she loves you. And personally, I think it's cruel of you to not give her what she wants. She deserves it."

"At the cost of being indelicate…" Vikas started but Kajal interrupted him.

"I know what you are going to say. I told you I was jealous of her or some such nonsense. I have told you many times, and I think I have proven to you that I am not that insecure, jealous bitch any more. And I suspect that you still think that I feel the same way about Pari. You had no problem in fucking those girls on the boat when I asked you to, but you are not doing Pari because you think she's the one I am jealous of. I am not. I swear to you that I am not."

"How do you know I am not doing her? Maybe I have been nailing her everyday?" Vikas suggested.

"If you have then that's great. I won't ask for her story, I consider her at the same level as me in your life." Kajal shook her head slowly "But somehow I don't think you are doing her. And she wants it badly."

"You know that for sure?"

"I do, and I am requesting you to take her."

"And you will be okay with that?"

"No. I will rejoice in that." She stood up, and leaned over Vikas, looking deep into his eyes "My dear owner, if you claimed her and asked her to live with us, I would not only accept it, I will love it. I like that girl very much. It makes me feel guilty that I got in her way by objecting to her before our marriage. She might have been your property by now if I hadn't got in the way."

"There is no need to feel guilty about that."

"I don't agree with you, Sir." She slowly rubbed his head, her fingers moving gently through his hair at the very base of his neck "And I do know how she took care of you when you and I were broken up, and I have seen with my eyes how much she has done not just for you but for me and my family. That girl is worth her weight in gold. She deserves to be your prized possession just as I am."

Vikas looked up "How do you know what happened when we were broken up?"

"I have never told you this," Kajal paused and took a deep breath " but Pari came to see me at mom's. She pleaded with me to take you back. She thought I had broken the engagement. She told me that if I had any doubts about her she would resign from the job and not tell you anything."

"What the fuck!"

Kajal nodded "Of course, I didn't tell her anything and I didn't take her offer. But she cured me of being a jealous bitch. I love you with all my life, every fibre of my being, every cell in my body, so I know that she doesn't love you more than I do, but she doesn't love you any less."

Reaching up with one hand, Vikas wiped her tears "I love you too, my darling. And yes, she is a great girl. I don't want to spoil her life by making her my possession as you suggest."

"You are too sweet, Patidev, and please don't get angry but you are making the same mistake that you were making in Rhea's case." Kajal got in his lap again "You may be giving her the greatest happiness she has always craved. And if you are worried about her marriage, I don't think you should be. If and when she's ready, she will go and get married. You would have given her some of the happiest memories of her life that she can look back on. If she's still got his unfulfilled desire with you, she might never want to marry because her head won't be clear."

"What if I make her my possession and she never wants to get married to anyone else?" Vikas asked thoughtfully.

"And what if she's so unhappy and unfulfilled by the fate of her first love that she is afraid to love again?" Kajal countered.

"Fuck! I never thought of that!" Vikas admitted.

Kajal's butt was resting on Vikas' cock and even as they were talking about the heavy-duty topics, his cock was getting hard form the heat of her firm, shapely ass cheeks rubbing on it.

"You are a sweet man," Kajal kissed his cheek "and you try to do the best for everybody, but you underestimate yourself. Your love, and guidance, may help Pari blossom in her own life. I don't mind if she stays your work wife, or your live-in property along with me, or your second wife…but I don't like you to treat her like only a secretary, especially because you think you are being kind but you are not."

"We live in India, honey," Vikas moved his hips a little and his thick cock, getting properly hard now started rubbing between Kajal's legs, on her pussy slit and ass crack "you can't have two wives here."

"That's all bullshit, my owner, and you don't need to marry her to have her as your live-in property, mmmm…" Kajal moved with his movements and started to grind her wet pussy on his hot, hard shaft "I know you are deflecting again, but I won't let you…I will keep nagging you like a normal wife…aaah!"

Vikas lifted her ass in his hands and pushed his dick inside her hot cunt that was already soaking wet.

"You are not a normal wife?" He asked as he pulled her close again.

"Mmmm, we both know I am your whore extraordinaire, Sir." Kajal said and started moving her hips to fuck herself on his massive cock.

He got up, keeping her impaled on his cock and laid her on the long sofa where they were fucking before. Kajal crossed her legs around his waist and hugged him tight with both arms. In this position, she knew, he was going to pound her ruthlessly. Her pussy was pulsing with anticipation.

She was right. Vikas started slowly but then quickly increased the speed of his strokes. Each of his strokes ground her back into the leather of the couch making her body slide up. Then he passed his arms under her shoulder blades and gripped her shoulders. Kajal knew what was coming. She gasped and clung to him tight like a monkey.

Using long, powerful strokes Vikas started really drilling his wife's tight, hot pussy, stretching her cunt with his massive cock. His thrusts were rocking her body but now she was trapped in his strong arms and each stroke pummelled her cunt incredibly deep. His cock was hammering into her cervix and Kajal was yelping and screaming uncontrollably.

"Oh, baby!" She yelped as he fucked her rough and hard.

"Mummy!" Kajal scream when Vikas' cockhead slammed into her cervix again "Oh God!"

His strokes hard and brutally deep, started to heat up her body where she could clearly see a hot explosion coming up. She moved her ass and pushed herself even deeper on his cock. The hurt was gone and his ruthlessly deep strokes were causing so much pleasure in her body that Kajal had her eyes closed and was begging him not to stop.

"Baby, fuck me! Fuck me hard! Take your whore, darling." She pleaded as she pushed her ass back and forth, massaging his throbbing cock with her cunt "Yes, baby. Own me! Break me! Ah!"

As her pussy exploded into a deliciously hot orgasm, Kajal surrendered her whole body in his arms and cried and screamed while he nailed her into the couch like a beast.

Kajal squeezed herself against him until her soft, firm tits were crushed on his bare, manly chest and her nipples were buzzing with electricity. She sucked his neck and kept her ankles crossed behind him so her legs were open and she was fully accessible for his cock to conquer. Her whole body was squirming under him and she was moaning continuously as her orgasm washed over her body like a hot wave all the way from head to toe and then back up again.

"Oh god, baby!" She moaned in his ear "You can't imagine how much I love your cock! You are my everything!"

Vikas continued fucking her with long deep strokes that elicited hot, passionate moans from her.

She put her lips to his ear and whispered "Sorry, baby, I was picturing you fucking that hot bitch Sony Charishta on the ship when I just came."

"Mmm, you are such a dirty whore, girl!" Vikas whispered as he started drilling her with harder, more powerful strokes again.

"Yes, baby. Aaah…I am your whore, baby!" Kajal moaned as she started moving her hips urgently, her pussy was throbbing and she was ready for her next orgasm.

But Vikas had other ideas. He slowed down his strokes which made Kajal dig her nails into his back and beg in his ear.

"Please don't stop, baby." She begged and pumped her hips furiously to get his cock deeper into her hungry cunt.

"Who is my whore, Kaju?" He whispered in her as he kissed her cheek and neck. He kept varying his strokes between hard, slow and fast. Kajal's excited body was going through a rollercoaster of heat and desire.

"I am your whore, Patidev." She moaned in his ear "I am your property. Please, please, let your whore cum, Sir!"

Vikas kept fucking her, keeping her on the edge without letting her explode "Who owns you, Kaju?" He whispered and sucked her earlobe. His hot breath was caressing Kajal's sweaty neck. The hot and cool sensation was driving her crazy with passion.

She pushed her firm, hot tits into his chest and breathed "I am yours. You own me. My body, mind, heart and soul, you own everything, my Master. Please allow your whore to cum, my sweet Master. Please!"

Pressing his lips on her soft, moist lips, Vikas kissed her hard and Kajal quickly opened her lips to accept his tongue into her mouth. As they kissed and sucked on each other's tongues, Vikas slowly speeded up his strokes, gradually pushing Kajal's body towards the edge again. She arched her back and took his massive cock fully deep into her cunt until it was hitting her cervix with each thrust.

He broke the kiss and said "Now!" making her strokes harder and faster into her wet, hot cunt "Cum for me, whore!"

The force of his strokes continued hard and his cock slammed her ass into the sofa again and again with loud, powerful thrusts. The wild, passionate, furious pace of the fucking led to both of them coming at the same time.

"Oh maa!" Kajal screamed as her pussy exploded so hard and she felt Vikas' throbbing cock erupt inside her at the same time. She pushed her ass up off the sofa like she wanted to take his cock right into her womb. The orgasm was rocking her body so hard she didn't have full control over her body. Vikas was drilling her right into the sofa, her body, trapped in his strong arms was taking the force of his strokes in an intoxicated state.

"Mmmm, baby. I love you, my love." She whispered again and again in his ear as her body convulsed under him. She could feel his cock pulsating inside her as it pumped his hot seed into her womb marking her so deep like only he could.

Again they kissed. This one was not as furious but it was coated with the sweet sensations of their shared orgasm, like a piece of a chocolate dipped in ice cream. Kajal sucked his tongue and swallowed his saliva as they pressed their lips so hard together even air could not pass. Their hot breaths blended together in an erotic mix while their naked bodies moved together on the sofa in the dance that transcends the body and rocks the soul.

It was a few minutes before Vikas carefully withdrew his cock from Kajal's soppy, wet cunt. She moaned as she got up on all fours and knelt between his legs with sore thighs and legs. She lovingly licked his cock clean and ate his cum while smiling up into his eyes.

"You do know you own me like a bitch, don't you?" Kajal said as she finished cleaning him and crawled up to lie on his chest.

"Well, I know you love my cock." Vikas said and put his arm around her so she wouldn't fall off. He pressed her naked body against him.

"I admit that I love your cock." Kajal said gently rubbing his dick with her leg "But it's you. You own me. Every inch of my body belongs to you, my mind, my heart, my soul all of it is yours. There is nothing in the world that you would say and I would not do."

He kissed her forehead "I love you too, my love. And I am incredibly proud of having you as my wife, and my possession."

They fell asleep like that and woke up two hours later when Vikas' left arm slipped off the sofa and the jerk woke them both up.

"Oh, God! I can't believe I fell asleep like that." Vikas said "What time is it?"

"I did too, honey." Kajal said "Let me up and I will check."

A moment later she said "It's almost midnight, baby. We didn't even have dinner. I am being such a bad wife."

He got up, walked up to her and kissed her softly "A bad wife, but a good whore."
He told her "Let's take a shower, then have some food. Then another session, in the bedroom this time."

"It's late, baby. You won't be able to get up in time for office in the morning." Kajal reminded him.

"Who cares? I am the boss!" He told her and slapped her bare ass "Get in the shower, slut."

Kajal wiggled her butt and went into the bathroom.

Chapter 29 – Parineeti Thinking About Vikas

Parineeti came out of the bathroom fully naked. Her body was still moist. She made sure that her bedroom door was locked. She turned off the lights and turned on a side table lamp that give a very limited light. She went to her dresser and took out a tshirt. It was Vikas' tshirt.

Usually Vikas played Squash in the evenings after work but in the summer the evenings were too warm so he would play in the early morning before office. The Squash club was close to the office so he would come to the office and shower there. It happened one time that Parineeti arrived at the office when he was in the shower. His discarded tshirt was lying on top of his Squash bag. Parineeti had picked it up and quickly put it in her desk drawer. Then in the evening after Vikas had gone home, she had stuffed the tshirt in her purse and brought it home.

It was about 3 months ago that she had liberated that tshirt but it still had the smell of Vikas' naked sweaty body very strongly in it. Parineeti slipped it on. It was loose on her body. She got between the covers. She felt between her legs. Her pussy was wet. One whiff of Vikas' tshirt could do that to her. She loved it.

She kept smelling the tshirt on her chest as she slowly rubbed her pussy. Today had been amazing. The kissing with Vikas had been a make-out session each time. He was beginning to feel more comfortable and free with her body. If this continued one day soon, he will simply take her. It was inevitable. She pushed one finger into her hungry, wet pussy.

The cotton tshirt was rubbing on her bare tits. She closed her eyes and imagined that it was Vikas wearing the tshirt who was pressing down on her hot, full tits. She moaned as she slipped another finger into her wet hole.

Vikas had definitely fucked that model hard. Parineeti could hear her yelps and screams from her office. It was a good thing. The more he did casual sex in his office, the sooner he would stop thinking that he could ruin Parineeti's life just by fucking her. And then…then, he would just take her. She wondered if she would scream like that. She probably would.

Parineeti rubbed her clit and pushed three fingers up into her cunt as she remembered how she had ridden Vikas' lap in the car. She didn't know how she had acted so boldly so close to her home. But he did drive her crazy like that.

She could smell his sexy, manly smell as she had sucked his tongue into her mouth. Her pussy got really hot as she thought about that moment. His smell from the tshirt made the scene so real in her mind.

As she thought about the moment when his warm fingertips had floated down her spine to her lower back, just a centimetre above her ass crack, her pussy exploded. She whimpered.

Biting her lip hard, Parineeti tried to keep the noise down as she surrendered to the intense orgasm. Her fingers worked fast and deep in her cunt. Her thumb was pressing and teasing her clit and her orgasm was carrying on long and delicious!

Her body collapsed back on the bed as she enjoyed the hot, slightly painful, aftershocks of that hot orgasm.

Each day she was getting closer to him. Kissing him good morning, sitting on his lap to take dictation, even introducing that hot girl to him so he could destroy her…it was all leading to only one thing. Pretty soon she would not just be his personal secretary, she would be his personal property.

When she was horny, she thought of herself as becoming his whore. Sometimes as she fingered her hot, hungry pussy she would call herself his bitch in her mind. She wondered what he would call her after he took her. She didn't care. As long she belonged to him, he could call her anything.

It's not that she had not thought about the flip side of it but she had not given it much probability. There was a small chance that he still may not fuck her. Remember what he had said in the restaurant? But it was a small chance.

One time, only one time, she needed to him to fuck her. After that his objections will be gone and he will accept her as his….let's say bitch. She knew she was pretty. She knew that he thought so too. Now that she was dressing bolder for him he was starting to admire her beauty even more. She would continue to be fully available to him 24/7. She was sure it would not take much for him to realise that she was born to be his property.

Going from there to cuddling with him in bed, and then…Parineeti's thoughts started to run away with her and her pussy started to get wet again. She decided to discipline herself and go to sleep instead. It still took her more than an hour to fall asleep. Her main thought as she fell asleep was that she would see Vikas again tomorrow. Parineeti tried to remember what time he was coming to office tomorrow. She was trying to recall his calendar when her brain turned off and she fell asleep.

Chapter 30 – Hina Enjoys Anticipation

Hina was well aware that this was her once in a lifetime chance. She decided to be bold and bet everything on it. It had been a long shot and now that the long shot had come in, it would be stupid not to grab it with both hands.

She had called her beautician on her mobile and made an emergency appointment for the morning. She could not afford to go to big beauty salons but the benefit was that she was friendly the beautician at the small salon and could twist her arm to squeeze her in at this short notice.

It was a good thing, she had the dress that he seemed to like. She wondered if she should dress bolder. She had some dresses that had no back at all, there was one that even showed a bit of her ass crack. But no, tomorrow is the first meeting, in his office. Better play it safe. And he had liked this dress based on Vansh's input so this was the dress to go in. Thankfully, Ruhi did have 8" high platform heels. They were black and black goes with everything.

After the dress, she had chosen her accessories, lipstick and lined up everything ready for tomorrow. She would call in sick to the restaurant. No point in fucking up her only chance by getting stuck somewhere. She would take out the last money in her bank account and pay for the beauty salon and a taxi. She could take the bus on the way back but getting there in pristine condition was paramount.

There was no question of wearing panties. Unlike Vansh, she knew how things worked and she had a good idea of how the meeting would go. If the boss liked her look, it was certain that he was going to do her. He might do her right there in his office or he might take her home later. No, no, he was married, so he would probably do her there or take her to a hotel. But there was no question in Hina's mind that she would be taking the boss' dick if things went well.

On the other hand, if he didn't try to fuck her that means she would not get any role. Her role will need to be earned by her pussy and if the boss didn't want her pussy, well, then there was no chance of her getting into modelling there. That is why she was going to do her very best to look totally fuckable.

Hina took her tablet and got into bed. She went to the VisCom site and looked in the staff section. It was not hard to find Vikas Malhotra. Hina was taken aback when she looked at his photo on his staff profile. Wow, he was so young. He was definitely a bit older than her, but as CEO's go he was very young. And he was handsome. Why, the man could model in his own projects. He had filmstar looks, nobody would say he worked behind a desk.

But other than the looks, Hina could sense his power also. He looked and smiled like a filmstar but there was that about him which confirmed her opinion that he would be in her tomorrow. Well, if he liked her looks in the first place. Looking at his picture, Hina very much wanted him to be in her. She was convinced that this man would own his secretary, no matter if he was married or not. Hina googled to find more pictures of him. She found quite a few, from corporate functions, company events, press releases, news articles, and as she scrolled down, she found a couple of them from a martial arts competition. In one of them he was fighting, in another one, he was holding a trophy.

Going back one, she again opened the one where he was dressed in a martial arts uniform. His right leg was pushed back and his hands were up in a fighting stance. She realised suddenly that she was wet. It looked like she had been wet for a while and just realised it when her pussy started leaking. Oh yes, Hina definitely wanted him in her tomorrow. She tried to think of some sentences that would allow her to let him know that she was interested and available. She thought back on how casting directors usually brought up this subject…no, they were usually too obvious or crass. Hina wanted to be classy and poised while gently hinting that if there was a position open to be his slut Hina wanted to apply for it.

She scrolled with one hand, letting her right hand slip between her legs. She was looking at his pictures but her mind was superimposing her own movie over it. She was imagining how he would take her in hand and bend her to his will with a firm hand.

Hina liked a strong hand, it made her feel safe and protected when a man took control of her and guided her where he wanted her. Unfortunately, she didn't meet many men like that. Even the casting directors who were strong and dominant in business, became eager to please when things went to the couch.

This was her one problem with her current boyfriend. Vansh was a great guy and she liked him a lot, but he was never the dominant type. She had tried to give him hints which he had not gotten, then she had told him outright that she wanted him to take charge in the bedroom. He had tried it, he had even spanked her once or twice but it was not his thing and Hina could feel that which led to her not being satisfied. Their sex was good because they were emotionally close but it never had the raw, savage quality that Hina craved. Still, he was a good boyfriend and loved Hina a lot.

Hina sighed and focused again on the man in the picture. Her pussy throbbed again. She came to a picture of a raft going through a white water rapid. Vikas' face was visible but just barely recognisable as it was an action shot. She saw it was from YouTube and clicked it to open the video that it was from. It was a short one minute video from an action cam that showed the raft going through a big rapid. At one point the person in front of Vikas bounced off the raft. Hina thought that it was a girl. As she went overboard, Vikas grabbed for her and got his fingers hooked into her life jacket. He pulled her in and held her on the edge of the raft until they were through the rapid. Then he helped her climb back in.

As Hina ran that twenty second part of the video repeatedly, her fingers were working in and out of her wet, soppy cunt. She touched her clit with her thumb and her body shook. She quickly went back from the video to the martial arts competition picture. Then she closed her eyes and lay back. She let her imagination run wild as she pushed two fingers into her pussy and fucked herself deep and fast. Her fingers were getting faster and harder. She could feel her pussy was telling her that it was ready to explode.

Keeping her eyes tightly closed, she let her mind change gears. In her mind, she visualised Vikas drilling her hard. His strokes got faster and faster, then suddenly, she let him cum in her. Hina's pussy erupted in a hot mess of her cum and a loud whimper came out of her mouth. She kept on fingerfucking her pussy while in her mind, Vikas filled her body with so much cum that it was dripping from her pussy hole. She sighed as she tried to catch her breath, letting her body slowly cool down.

She couldn't wait for the next day to dawn.

Chapter 31 – Vikas Meets with Shilpa

"Vikas, you never give me credit for all the preparations I do, this is a tough job, buddy." Shilpa Shetty said.

"Darling, you are the boss, you run the company, I bet you have people to blow on your nails when you want to dry your nail polish." Vikas said.

They were sitting around the conference table at Crewing Partners. There were a few other people sitting around the table, but mostly they were busy reading some documents, using their phones or looking at the girl in the corner.

"Oh, you think I can't even blow?" Shilpa looked right into his eyes.

"How would I know that?" Vikas replied and leaned in, he placed his hand on her shoulder and whispered in her ear "You are looking dynamite, by the way."

"Thanks, but what's the use?" She said in a low voice "Not like anything has any effect on you."

"You never know, you have never looked this ravishing before." Vikas smiled "It's a stunning dress."

Shilpa was a mature beauty who looked much younger for her age and had the slim, toned body that most 22-year olds would envy. She was wearing a sleeveless silver silky gown with a very deep neck and a wrap around skirt part that bared her right leg all the way to her thigh joint. The neck was wide enough to show a big part of her cleavage. The sleeves were cut deep enough to bare her armpits. Her shaved armpits were visible every time she moved her hands. The dress was tight on her flat stomach but draped beautifully around her hips and legs.

The fabric of her dress had a dotted inline texture which didn't do much to cover the translucent nature of the thin cloth. It was a mix of silk and synthetic that shimmered in the light and slithered against her skin in a very mouth-watering display. The gown had a back that was cut so deep that wearing a bra was not possible. It was not hard to guess that she was not wearing anything under the thin, clinging dress, even a thong would have been visible. Shilpa had a beautiful face with sharp features and she knew that her beauty intimidated most men. She never hesitated to use that to her advantage. Her perfectly shaped lips were painted dark red and her hair was loose on her shoulders and back.

Her heels were 6" high mules, much more suitable for a fashion show runway than a corporate office. She always dressed too sexy for office and her staff followed her example. Looking at her nobody would say that she was married. Not that she cared. It was common knowledge in Crewing Partners that while her husband Raj Kundra Shetty owned the company as a director, Shilpa owned her husband. Not even a blade of grass in the CP lawn could move without her permission.

Vikas had been a client of her company for several years and they had developed a good friendship. She always flirted boldly with him but while he flirted back just as boldly, he had never made a real move on her. There were rumours that Shilpa used her feminine charms to further her business. While some people thought she teased and flirted with clients, others claimed that Shilpa's legs were always open for their best clients. Nobody knew the strict truth.

"You do know there's nothing under the dress, don't you?" She whispered to Vikas.

"I disagree." Vikas grinned "I think there's the best merchandise under the dress."

"Are you in the market?" Shilpa raised an eyebrow.

Before Vikas could answer, a girl who had been fiddling with a laptop on a table in the front corner of the room, approached the conference table.

"I am ready, Ma'am." She said to Shilpa.

Vikas looked at the girl, she was very beautiful with a longish, slightly dusky face, big beautiful eyes and plump lips that invited dirty, depraved thoughts. Her dark hair was loose and framed her small face in a very photogenic manner. She was wearing a black tube top with a beige formal jacket over it. Her wrap-around skirt was matching the jacket and went halfway to her knees. She was wearing 6" stilettos. Vikas let his eyes inspect her fully, from her shapely, bare legs, to her flat belly visible below the tube top, to her chest visible in the open jacket, above the tube top.

Shilpa nodded "Vikas, you know Pooja Hegde, she will lead the presentation today."

"Yes, I do. Nice to see you, Pooja." Vikas said.

"Thank you, Sir, I mean nice to, have you, I mean.." She stopped "Can I start, please?"

Vikas nodded "Take it away."

Everybody pulled their chairs forward towards the table. Pooja turned off the room lights. The curtains were already drawn. She pressed a button on her laptop and the first slide was projected on the main screen facing the conference table, opposite where Vikas was sitting.

"Crewing Partners, your partner in growth." The title slide said.

Keeping his face towards the screen, Vikas dropped his left hand under the table and placed it lightly on Shilpa's leg. Her right leg was closest to him and it was bare to the hip in her bold, sexy gown. His fingers touched the smooth skin of her thigh. He caressed there softly by moving just his fingers and not letting his arm move. Shilpa continued to look at the screen but under the table she opened her legs wider. This pulled her skirt open even more and Vikas had more access to her thigh. He continued to caress her smooth, silky thigh slowly.

Pooja led the presentation expertly. She went into details of camera crews they hired, their experience, their qualifications and their skill. She talked about how Crewing Partners made these crews available to other agencies like VisCom who could use them on specific project without have to pay salaries for those times when there were no projects.

While Pooja was presenting a case study of how much it would cost VisCom to employ a crew on a salary basis, Vikas was noticing her long legs and her tight butt in her form-fitting miniskirt. He noted how comfortably she was pacing back and forth on her high heels as she made a point and turned to Vikas then moved back to the laptop. Her eye contact was great, and Vikas looked right into her eyes as he moved his hand along Shilpa's bare thigh. He moved his fingers slowly down following the curve of her shapely, smooth thigh.

Reaching down casually, Shilpa took Vikas' hand and moved it higher along her leg. As his palm rested on her inner thigh, the tip of his little finger touched her pussy slit. It got wet in her cunt juices. Vikas continued to slowly caress her thigh and traced her pussy slit with the fingernail of his little finger. Her pussy lips parted and closed as his finger moved up and down.

Shilpa squirmed as Pooja was demonstrating in her presentation how Crewing Partners could grow and provide support to VisCom in their expansion. Vikas was tracing the very tip of Shilpa's pussy hole and dipping his fingertip inside her soaking wet cunt. Shilpa was keeping a control on her breathing but her heartbeat was rising fast. She squirmed a little again as Vikas's finger moved up and parted her pussy lips more. Then she almost let out a yelp as his fingernail touched her clit. She bit her bottom lip and suppressed the noise before it could get out.

As Pooja displayed the final "Questions?" slide, Vikas pulled his hand out from between Shilpa's legs and placed it back on the table.

Pooja turned on the lights and faced the table. She looked at Vikas expectantly.

"Thank you, Pooja," Vikas said "that was a great presentation, and covered a lot of information that I wanted. I can see you did a lot of homework and put everything in one place in one easy to digest package. Great job. Very impressive."

"You are welcome, Sir, thank you." Pooja smiled.

Vikas nodded "You talked about certifications and such for the camera crews you hire. Do you know what level that goes to, is all the crew certified or a certain level?"

"Sir, usually the cinematographers and DOPs are certified, electricians and other such members are certified for their respective trades and for health and safety regulations."

"Makes sense." Vikas nodded "The salary data that you used for the full-time crew, could you tell me how you calculated those?"

"Yes Sir, those are the minimum salaries approved by the unions and the government."

"Good. And are those the salaries that Crewing Partners pays them?" Vikas asked.

A guy on Vikas' right started to answer. Pooja quickly raised her hand slightly, shutting him up before he could say anything. She herself stayed quiet and looked at Shilpa.

Shilpa laughed and slapped Vikas' shoulder "Vikas, you naughty boy. She can't tell you that, that's confidential HR data."

Vikas laughed "Smart girl."

Pooja smiled.

"I have some more questions but they are regarding commercials so I am going to keep them for Shilpa. Thank you, Pooja."

"You are welcome, Sir." Pooja smiled again.

"Let's go to my office." Shilpa said, standing up "Thank you, everybody."

Chapter 32 – Vikas and Shilpa's Private Meeting

While Shilpa closed the door, Vikas went around the desk and sat in her chair. She walked over to him and perched on the desk near him. Vikas moved slightly and pointed to the space next to him. Shilpa lifted her foot and placed it where he indicated. Her gown skirt opened at the hip, baring her whole leg and even a little sliver of her pantyless pussy. Vikas slowly caressed her leg, his hand moving up along her calf to the back of her knee.

"I want her, who is she?" He said.

"You have seen her before, she is Gulshan's team member. Gulshan is on holiday so I asked her to do the presentation." Shilpa said "I am sure she will be happy to spread her legs for you. I saw how she was looking at you. I won't even have to say 'be good to the client'".

"No, you didn't get me." Vikas moved his hand along her thigh, feeling the silky smoothness of her skin "We have never had such a good presentation in any of my meetings with you. Gulshan used to talk from a small notepad he carried into the meeting. I want her to join my company. Send her for an interview."

"You want to steal her from me?" Shilpa widened her eyes dramatically "How dare you, Mr. Malhotra?"

Vikas let his hand linger on her upper thigh and rubbed slowly "You just said she's just a team member."

"But she's a good team member. Very valuable to me."

"You are deliberately trying to drive a hard bargain." Vikas said "Name your price."

Shilpa leaned over him and looked into his eyes, her lips barely an inch from his lips "You want her, I want you."

Vikas grinned "So, I get her and get to bang you in the bargain? I would be stupid to say no to that."

"Good. Deal?"

"No!" Vikas pushed her foot off the chair and stood up. He stood close to her with his body pressing against her. He took her hands and pushed them behind her back. He held both her wrists in one hand and grabbed her hair with the other hand.

"Ah!" Shilpa moaned as he jerked her head up.

He leaned closer and looked into her eyes "Once I take you, you belong to me. I will fuck you every time we meet. I don't care if you come to my office with your husband for a business meeting or I come across you in an art gallery benefit, when I see you I am going to nail you."

Shilpa breathed heavily "To use your words, I would be stupid to say no to that."

Vikas pressed his lips hard on her soft, red lips and kissed her with his tongue already slipping into her mouth. Shilpa pressed back against his mouth with an eager enthusiasm and opened her lips, readily surrendering to his tongue. She made no effort to free her hands or her hair as they shared a hot, wet kiss. She kept her lips sealed against his and drank his saliva hungrily.

"Then deal." Vikas said as he slowly broke the kiss and stepped back, freeing her from his grip.

Shilpa reached behind her back and pulled open a fastening that contained four hooks. As she unwrapped that her dress fell open easily. She dropped it on the chair and said "Where do you want me?" She pointed to the sitting area "That couch is quite big."

Vikas unzipped his pants and took out his cock. It was almost fully erect.

"Oh God!" Shilpa moaned as she saw his thick, massive dick.

He took her hair in his hand again and said "Bend over."

"Y...yes, yes, Sir." She trembled a little as she turned under his guidance and placed her hands on her desk.

"Lower, baby, much lower, you'll need the support, believe me."

"Oh God." Shilpa moaned again. Vikas kept pressing her down until she put her upper body on the glass desk and her tits were pressed on it.

Vikas took her hips in his hands, placed his cockhead on her pussy and pushed once. Her body jerked forward with pain as his swollen cockhead stretched her little hole and popped into her tight cunt.

He kept his grip and pushed in deeper.

"Ah god!" She screamed as several thick, throbbing inches of Vikas' massive dick invaded her tight cunt with a painful stroke.

Raj Kundra Shetty walked into the outer cabin of his wife's office suite and said hello to her personal secretary.

"Good morning, Huma."

Huma Qureshi looked up from her computer and said hello to the director "Good morning, Sir."

"Is madam free?" He asked. He could be her husband and director of the company but he would not dare enter his wife's private cabin without permission.

"Sorry, Sir, she's in a private meeting with a client."

"Oh, with whom?"

Huma hesitated a second then said "VisCom CEO Mr. Vikas Malhotra, Sir."

Raj had met Vikas before, handsome, young CEO, very dynamic and powerful. VisCom was their biggest client. He nodded.

"I will wait." Raj said.

For a second, Huma looked like she was about to advise him against it, but then she just said "Yes, Sir."

Raj took a seat on one of the visitor chairs and picked up a magazine from a side table.

"Ah God!" Shilpa's voice came loud and clear from inside. Raj squirmed. It became clear what kind of private meeting his wife was having with the young, dashing CEO.

Inside, Vikas held her shoulders and told Shilpa "Spread wider, baby, it's going to hurt some more."

"Fuck!" Shilpa breathed but she nodded and opened her legs wider. It seemed to relieve the pressure inside her pussy a little bit.

Vikas pulled out a little and pushed in again, going a little deeper this time. Shilpa moaned. Vikas kissed her cheek and kept her in control by pressing his hand down on her back, crushing her soft firm tits on the glass as he fucked her tight cunt in and out. Shilpa moaned with each stroke of his cock in her pussy but she yelped every time he pushed in harder and conquered fresh territory inside her.

Raj squirmed as he heard those yelps. It was evident that the client CEO was fucking his wife who was CEO of Crewing Partners. But Raj didn't have a choice except to sit there and wait, while he listened to his wife being fucked by the other guy. He wondered idly what would happen if he impulsively burst into the room while they were having sex. He knew she would not be embarrassed. She would definitely not stop. Depending on her mood, she might tell him to get out or shut up and watch. His dick stirred in his pants as he thought about sitting in the visitor's chair and watching the dominant CEO pound his wife hard as he seemed to be doing now based on her screams and yelps from inside.

Shilpa could feel her nipples hard as they grated on the glass. Her legs were open as wide as they could go and still Vikas' dick was fitting very tightly in her pussy, stretching her to the limit. She was breathless and very hot. Her whole body was feeling the rush of sensations caused by his hard cock. In her marriage, Shilpa controlled everything, but here Vikas had taken her control away right from the first step. She had never felt that dominant, strong control of a real man ever since she stopped living with her father years ago. That feeling of being in the power of a strong man was making Shilpa feel about eighteen years old and fully helpless. It was so arousing that not just her pussy but her entire body felt like it was soaking in the delicious juices of desire and passion.

Vikas was drilling her with a smooth rhythm of long, hard strokes now. His long, thick shaft was reaching deep into Shilpa's tight pussy. The massive beast had opened her up with sustained, repeated assaults and her pussy was wrapped around his throbbing meaty pole now like a stretched latex glove.

"Ah, mumma!" Shilpa screamed as Vikas' long, powerful cock slammed into her cervix and made her body reverberate with an electric pain.

Huma carefully kept her eyes on her monitor but she crossed her legs and squeezed her thighs tightly. She knew her boss fucked other men than her husband but she had never heard noises like this coming from her cabin before. It was like Huma could visualise the whole scene in her mind by following the sounds. She could easily guess that Shilpa was bent over her own desk and the client CEO was pounding her from behind.

Not that Huma would mind it herself. She had fantasized more than once about the dashing CEO coming to meet Shilpa and fucking Huma at her desk. Huma had scheduled today's meeting herself and in anticipation she had worn a super tight red minidress which squeezed her big boobs together and up for a drool-worthy cleavage effect. Huma had a beautiful face and a nicely proportioned body with long, sexy legs. But she was the opposite of her boss Shilpa Shetty. While Shilpa was slim to the point of looking hungry, Huma was healthy and heavy. She was by no means fat, but she was not what one would call a typical model. She liked to wear tight, and when possible, revealing clothes to show off her sexy, fair body and she did get some male attention but nothing compared to her boss.

Unlike most visitors, Vikas usually took a minute or two to stop by Huma's desk after a meeting with Shilpa and flirted with her a little bit in a sweet, safe kind of way. He always commented on her dress or shoes and Huma always made sure to wear something really nice and sexy when she knew Vikas was coming for a meeting the next day. Today's dress was her boldest yet. It was not super short but it did show Huma's long, healthy legs and part of her thighs. Her best feature was her breasts and she had worn a demi-cup bra today to push them up for a close inspection. Her dark red lipstick matched her dress and her shoes which were 5" high pumps. Huma had learnt already that men loved long legs in high heels even if they were thick thighs like hers. She could walk in high heels like normal because of the practice she had put in them. Her body was a natural heavy but she kept it toned with regular workouts and her core was very strong.

Huma knew that her boss had had a crush on Vikas and she definitely could not compete with her but nothing was stopping Huma from flirting with the handsome CEO. He always responded well and Huma usually got flushed with his remarks. From his comments so far she knew he didn't mind that she was more curvy than most girls and wouldn't mind doing her. But that was just flirting which he did in a clever, witty style. Although in her fantasies, he had fucked her many times at her desk, in her home, and many other places, in reality, he had never touched her. But then he had never fucked Shilpa either so maybe things were changing because he was definitely giving her a good banging today from the sound of it.

Shilpa was indeed having the time of her life, bent over her own desk and pounded by Vikas' hard, brutal cock as it ripped through her. She clawed the desk as she felt the sexual tension mounting in her body and then suddenly her back arched and her body went stiff like a board.

"Oh god!" She screamed loudly as everything released like her boat had just met a colossal wave and it had soaked her all the way through, inside and out.

Her moans that followed the loud, long scream were just as loud, but rhythmic and throaty. Her slim, sexy body was being ripped to shreds by the savage orgasm and Shilpa was crying and screaming without a care for who could hear her. She had no thought in her mind except Vikas' dick which was fucking her brains out. Her tits grinding hard on the glass were causing even more sensations in her slender body and Shilpa was way out of control. Her eyes were leaking tears on the glass, and her knees were not able to support her weight. Her whole body was now supported by the desk as Vikas pumped her hard, making her smooth, sweaty body grind back and forth on the smooth glass.

Raj Kundra buried his face in the magazine so the secretary could not see his expression but he had to cross his legs when he heard that loud, long scream from his wife's office. He could not help that his dick was getting hard even as he was listening to his wife getting fucked by some other guy. Raj had heard the rumours that Shilpa got intimately involved with some of the clients but this was the first time when he was personally present in the outer office while she was getting the shit fucked out of her in her private office. He squeezed his legs to hide his hard-on.

It wasn't that difficult. Although Shilpa called him "pencil-dick Kundra", in all fairness his dick was not as thin as a pencil. It was definitely not particularly thick or long, just not quite as thin as a pencil. When they fucked he never needed to ask her if she came. He knew she didn't. She never did with him. That's why she had a drawer full of sex toys. While he was thankful that she let him fuck her from time to time, he knew it was not his looks or sexual prowess that she had fallen for. It was his money. And if he could not provide her that for some reason, he knew well that she would leave him in a Bombay second.

There was no need for Raj to worry about Huma. She had troubles of her own and wasn't bothered about him. She had started to get wet the moment she had heard that first scream of Shilpa that told her that Vikas had entered her. Her pussy had only gotten wetter since and now her panties were soaked. The little lace thong she had worn this morning thinking it was sexy, was drenched in her cunt juices and was rubbing on her pussy, making her even hotter. She could not squeeze her thighs any more because her thong would be wrung out and soak her chair in pussy juices. Her breath was heavy and hot, while she was moving her fingers on the keyboard in an attempt to look busy, she was typing literally non-sense.

Vikas pushed his fingers deep into Shilpa's silken locks again and held her down, pressing her cheek to her desk he fucked her so hard that her body slammed into the desk producing a rhythm of hard, thumping noises with the same speed as his cockhead was pummelling her cervix. Shilpa got power at home but not sexual satisfaction. For that, she usually went out to clubs, flirted with employees and even mingled with strangers in certain specific situations. But this was different. Vikas was a man she met regularly for business, she knew he was recently married and he knew that she was married. He had already made it clear that he was taking control of her which meant he would fuck her whenever he wanted and Shilpa would have no control over it. This thought, combined with the expertise with which he was crushing her on her own desk was making Shilpa so helplessly turned on that she could feel her next orgasm building up right on the heels of the first one.

"Yes, Vikas, chodo, zor se chodo." She was crying out for him to fuck her even harder, without caring that her office was not soundproof and her secretary Huma could probably hear everything. Oh God, she had told Raj they would go for lunch together after the meeting. He never dared to be late for an appointment with her, which meant that he was outside, listening to her screams while her client's dick was destroying her married pussy like a battering ram. Shilpa came even harder than the first time. This time she was imagining her husband's face as she screamed loudly several times, with her body rocking on the desk, completely out of her control.

Huma could feel her skin getting moist with sweat. She could clearly hear what was going on in Shilpa's office and her imagination was creating a picture from the sounds. She could see that Vikas was not fucking her like she had been fucked in her office before, instead he was systematically breaking her down and owning her. Shilpa's repeated grunts and loud screams were evidence that he was succeeding. Huma was very worried as to what it was doing to her mind. She was in a heightened state of arousal without anyone touching her and it was already changing her perspective of reality. She was getting so mesmerised by the thought of Vikas' cock that she was afraid when Vikas came out, she might just go down on her knees and beg him to destroy her the same way he had destroyed Shilpa.

She stole a glance towards Shilpa's husband. His face was covered by the magazine. She knew he could hear the noises from Shilpa's private office as well. If anything, he could hear them better, sitting closer to the office. Huma knew the status of their marriage. Shilpa didn't speak very highly of her husband and Huma had stolen enough glances at his crotch area to know why. Had he been able to satisfy Shilpa's incredible sexual hunger, she would not be the slut that she now was. Huma had gone clubbing with Shilpa and her sister a few times. It was hard to judge which one was a bigger slut but both went out only with the purpose to find cock. The problem was that they usually got it and Huma suffered in comparison by standing close to them.

Huma perked up her ears as she heard some different sounds from the private cabin of her boss. Some scuffling of feet, following by a fresh, loud scream from Shilpa and then the rhythmic noise of hard strokes. Huma guessed that they had changed position and now Vikas was fucking Shilpa from the front because the rhythmic thumping noise sounded like flesh on flesh. Huma was afraid he would not leave her fit to walk.

Vikas had indeed pulled out of Shilpa and turned her to face him. Then he pushed her back until her ass was perched on the desk and pushed into her cunt again, only much harder this time, sinking the whole length of his massive beast into her soft, delicate cunt with one brutal thrust.

"Aah, mar gayee!" Shilpa screamed as the swollen cockhead hit her cervix in the first ruthless stroke itself. Her body vibrated with the pain of his rough entry and she lowered her head on his shoulder to take support. He grabbed her by the hair and pulled her face up. Pressing his hot, demanding lips on her soft, red lips, he kissed her passionately with a fierce roughness to it. Shilpa opened her lips quickly and accepted his tongue into her mouth.

In the course of the long and sustained fucking, Shilpa had already cum three times with several small orgasms around the three big ones. And now as he drove into her cunt from the front, Shilpa wanted it badly. She rode his wonderfully thick and long cock, moving her ass like a wanton whore. She loved to dance. It was part of her fitness regime. Now she used those dancer's hips to grind against him, massaging his throbbing cock with her cunt walls as she used her pussy muscles to squeeze his meaty rod. Then he brought one hand between them and squeezed her breast. Shilpa lost control.

"Ungharaah!" Her scream was a mixture of a gasp, a scream and a grunt as her pussy exploded around Vikas' massive cock.

Raj took out his hankie and wiped his brow. He could not help it. It was too much for him to handle. When they fucked, which was rare, Raj could mostly last for a minute or two on rare occasions. He used to think that was normal. His brother Rohit had told him the same thing. But here this guy had been fucking her for ages and still wasn't close to finishing.

Thinking about his brother Rohit Shetty made Raj think about Shilpa's sister Shamita whom he was married to. Shamita was a beauty like Shilpa only even younger. But Rohit also had the same problem that Raj had. In the boardroom he was the king, but in the bedroom, not so much. Raj liked Shamita, she was nice to him and flirted with him a lot. It didn't mean she would have sex with him as both sisters shared all details about their husbands with each other. Shamita was as much of a slut as Shilpa was and when they went out to clubs as a foursome, both girls boldly looked for cocks even with their husbands around. Raj had lost count of how many times they had ditched them to go towards the toilets or the back alley with a stranger.

But they usually came back within a few minutes, not like this CEO who seemed to be intent on breaking Shilpa and not leave her fit enough to stand on her own feet. The rhythmic thumping noises coming from inside told him that they were probably fucking face to face now. He remembered Shilpa's gorgeous face. He was not allowed to kiss her except as needed to keep appearances in public. He could not even imagine having her beautiful mouth on his dick. The first time he had asked, she had laughed at him and told him to stop dreaming.

Still, he had had one blow job from her on one of her birthdays when he had bought her a diamond necklace. It had been a great 30 seconds of Raj's life. He could not help it, she just turned him on so much.

Vikas' tongue was fucking that hot mouth in and out as he fucked her hard and rough. His right hand was holding her hair, keeping her in his grip as his left hand kneaded her hot, firm tits rough, making her moan and yelp. Then he slowed down his rhythm and used rough, brutally deep battering ram strokes.

"Ah! Ah! Ah!" Each stroke made Shilpa cry out loudly.

"Oh ma!" She screamed as he came inside her, his massive cock throbbing so hard in her cunt that she could not control herself and came with him. He grabbed her ass cheeks, lowered her back on the desk and drilled her hard, pumping his hot, potent seed into her cunt from an angle that was sure to blaze a trail through her body and brand her womb. Shilpa whimpered helplessly as she felt him mark her so deep like that. There was absolutely no question of using a condom with a man like him. Shilpa simply wrapped her open legs around his waist and accepted his seed in her womb, while he continued to slam her into the desk.

She had no doubt that this man had claimed her completely like her husband had never managed to. She could not see a situation where she would be able to say no to anything he ordered. His hot, potent seed flooding her womb was evidence that she was his bitch now. Shilpa panted on the desk, her bare back, sweaty and slippery on the glass while her legs were wrapped around his waist. He was still sawing in and out of her cunt and Shilpa was loving the way his dick pulsed inside her, making her whole body pulse with it.

Huma's breath got stuck in her throat when she heard Shilpa's screams as she came on Vikas' cock. She felt sure that she knew the exact moment when Vikas came in her boss' cunt. Huma wondered what it would feel like to have his powerful seed flowing through her pussy. Her panties were totally soaked now and were wetting her thighs. There was nothing she could do. She was helpless. He was nowhere close to her and she was already helpless. Huma had no illusion about herself, she knew very well that if Vikas wanted her, she would get naked and spread her legs for him at one little gesture of his finger.

The silence after the loud screams was quite surprising. Raj could not understand but Huma knew that Shilpa must be sucking him clean right now. When the thought of his gorgeous wife's mouth wrapped around another man's cum-soaked cock occurred to Raj, he squirmed uncomfortably on the chair. Would she do it? No, there was no way. She didn't like having her luscious lips touching a penis. She was much too classy for that.

As Vikas pulled his cum-drenched cock out of Shilpa's tight, used, messy cunt, he pulled her closer to the edge of the desk. There with her hot, slender body completely naked on the edge of her own desk, Vikas rubbed his cock on her tits and on her chest between her tits. Shilpa moaned as she felt how he was marking his territory. Yes, she was his territory. He had just invaded her and conquered her. Now he was planting his flag. Shilpa felt a thrill that flooded her body like electric buzz as she felt his control and authority marked on her so definitely and irrevocably.

He slowly pulled her down and guided her down to her knees. Shilpa didn't protest at all as he brought her face between his legs and told her to lick it clean without using any words.

While Raj was debating outside the office if his classy wife could bring herself to touch a man's penis with her mouth, inside the office, the classy wife Shilpa Shetty was looking up into Vikas' eyes as she sucked his cock clean with her beautiful mouth and ate his cum. Her soft, plump lips were wrapped around his shaft and she was moving her head back and forth taking it into her mouth. His cum tasted amazing to her and it showed in the way she ate it all and went to lick his balls in search for more. After she licked it all up, she looked up at him to see if she could get up

Instead of letting her up, Vikas pointed down. Shilpa looked down and saw many splashes of cum on his shoes. Her face flushed. She looked up at him and said "Really?"

She waited a second for his answer but when he didn't say anything, she surrendered. Nodding her head to show her assent, she bent over low on her hands and knees, bringing her face close to his feet. Then, she slowly licked up the drops of cum. They had the same amazing taste and Shilpa eagerly picked one after the next. When she licked them all up, she saw the streaks left on his leather shoes by her tongue. This time, she didn't wait for him to tell her. She simply lowered her head and evened things out by flattening her tongue and licking around the shoes.

"Happy?" She said as she sat back on her knees and looked up at him.

Cupping her soft cheek in his warm hand, Vikas smiled into her eyes "That's like a good bitch."

A pink tinge coloured Shilpa's fair cheeks as she realized how proud she felt from his dirty, degrading comment. Her tits were firm again and her nipples were erect and buzzing.

"Thank you, Sir." She smiled back, knowing well that he had just claimed her and they both knew it.

Chapter 33 – Raj Joins the Client Meeting

"Sir?" Huma looked at Raj "Ma'am has messaged that you may go in now." She relayed the message that Shilpa had sent on the inter-office chat app.

"Oh, thank you." Raj got up. In the last few minutes of silence, Raj's erection had gone down. It wasn't big to start with but now nothing showed in his pants as he got up and walked to the door of his wife's private cabin.

Huma wondered if she should take the chance to go to the toilet to discard her panties and wipe her pussy. But if Vikas came out and went in that time, she would be kicking herself for weeks. She looked down between her legs. Her panties were so soaked that they were wetting her chair. Thankfully, the dress had ridden up when she sat so there was no wet patch on it. When Raj opened the door and walked in, Huma saw that Vikas was sitting in a visitor chair. Huma estimated that she had about two minutes. She picked up her purse and quickly walked to the private bathroom that her boss had allowed her to use. It was within the office suite.

Raj was uncertain how to approach the situation, but Shilpa was quite at ease. She came out from her seat and hugged him. "Hi baby!" She kissed him on the lips. Raj got a weird taste from her lips. And he was very sure she smelled of cum. In fact, the whole office smelled strongly of sex and cum.

Ignoring the smells with an effort, Raj smiled and hugged his wife. Damn, she looked amazing in that dress. She looked hot in any dress, in fact. Raj watched her tight ass in the thin dress as she walked back to her seat.

"You know Mr. Malhotra, of course." Shilpa indicated Vikas with a gesture.

"Of course, of course." Raj stepped over to him and shook hands "Hello Mr. Malhotra, nice to see you again."

"Please call me Vikas." Vikas smiled as he shook hands.

Raj sat down in the chair next to Vikas.

"Baby, Vikas is expanding his business and we have been talking some terms about how we can help him in crewing for the growing number of projects."

"That is fantastic. I am happy that our collaboration grows, Mr. Malhotra, I mean Vikas."

"Me too, Raj, but it depends on if your wife cooperates."

"Oh, is she not?" Raj asked.

"He is talking about the new terms, honey." Shilpa looked at Raj, then said to Vikas "I will send you those estimates, Sir, and we can have another meeting next week. I know you like to drive a hard bargain but I can assure you that I will cooperate. Me, my company and my staff is at your disposal. We want to keep you happy."

"Well, that reassures me some, but I do want to see the figures. Please send me those and let's have another meeting next week."

"I will get my secretary to talk to your girl." Shilpa said.

"Make sure you allow enough time for that meeting, today's demo was ok, but next time…well, as you said, I will drive a hard bargain and you might find yourself surrendering to my demands."

Shilpa smiled "When did I say no to your demands, Sir? As I said, it is our endeavour to please you."

Raj wasn't sure if they were talking in such double entendres or his mind was dirty but all he could get was that Vikas was telling his wife he would fuck her again and harder next week. She was agreeing in front of him. Raj squirmed in his seat.

Chapter 34 – Huma Uses the Copy Machine

Huma straightened up in her seat as Vikas came out of Shilpa's office and walked directly towards her desk. She had gone to the toilet and discarded her soaked panties. She had also wiped her pussy and thighs which were soaked in pussy juices. But while she was sitting there waiting for him to come out, Huma had become wet again. This time there were no panties in the way to soak up the juices if she started leaking.

"Either I am hungry because it's lunch time or you look really delicious today." He said as he stopped in front of her.

She flushed and managed to say "Thank you, Sir. You are very sweet."

He placed a hand on her desk and leaned in closer "And you, my dear Huma, look very spicy."

Getting bolder by his approach, Huma leaned in as well "Can you handle the spicy, Sir?"

"We can't say without tasting, can we?" Vikas let her see that she was checking her out. His eyes lingered on her big boobs in the deeply off-shoulders, red minidress, then moved back up to her eyes.

"Are you the kind who can taste and put it back?" Huma squeezed her boobs together by moving her arms, offering them up for his inspection.

"Better to inspect the dish before you sink your teeth into it."

"You are welcome to inspect as much as you like, Sir, or have a taste." Huma smiled, hoping he was getting that she was not just flirting but was actually available for him.

"Why don't you do me a favour, darling," He picked up a random paper from her desk and handed it to her "make a copy of this for me, will you?"

Huma took the paper, it was next week's cafeteria menu that had come for Shilpa's approval. Vikas would have absolutely no use for it. But Huma knew what he was asking. She walked around her desk and went to the copy machine in the corner. The large printer copier was only for use by Shilpa's office and since she didn't have a huge amount of copying to do, the machine usually just sat idle in a corner, turned on but not in use. Kind of like herself, Huma thought as she approached it.

She put the paper in the copier and bent over low to get the blank paper from the bottom tray even though that was not suitable for this paper. But she bent over low, keeping her legs open wide and her knees locked. Vikas stood a few feet behind her and watched. She looked damn hot in the tight dress. The totally unofficial high heels, her long, thick, legs bare to the thighs and the thin dress stretched taut across her tight butt. The high heels were pushing her ass back and up, Huma made sure to stay bent over longer than necessary so Vikas could get a good look. He had never done this kind of thing with her before and it was making Huma incredibly hot as this flirting moved into uncharted territory. The short dress was riding up her thighs and she was not sure if it was still covering her pussy.

Even if the dress were flashing her bare pussy as Vikas, Huma would not mind. Even if he were to step closer and jam his cock into her cunt, she would simply grab the paper tray and hold on while he fucked her. That thought was making her already wet pussy even hotter and wetter. Huma stood up and did the copy. She took the original and copy out and left them on the machine. She and Vikas both didn't have any use for them.

"I think I will need one more copy, darling." Vikas said.

"Yes, Sir." Huma turned again and repeated the procedure. This time though she was sure that her pussy was leaking on her thighs and that her dress was not covering her pantyless pussy. She kept her legs open wide and let him have a full look before standing up again to do the copy.

Vikas stepped closer before she could turn. Huma took out the original and the copy. She placed them on top of the machine and stood there, with her hands on the machine. As Vikas stepped even closer, she could feel his manly, hard body pressing lightly on her body from behind. His breath was hot on her bare back and Huma was afraid she might start moaning any moment. He slipped his arm around her midriff and pressed her back into him, his hand resting on her belly, just below her breasts. Huma shamelessly pressed her ass back into his crotch and let him take the lead on whatever he wanted to do to her.

"Let's compare them." He kept her in his grip and lined up the pages on top of the printer with his left hand.

"Yes, Sir." Huma said, her words choking in her throat. Her breath was heavy and she knew her big breasts were heaving with her breath.

He rested his chin on her bare shoulder and she could feel his stubble scratching her shoulder and the side of her neck. She turned her face slightly and pressed her cheek to his cheek as well. His stubble felt rough on her smooth cheek. She loved it.

Vikas pointed to one of the copies "Why is there this blank space, hon?"

"I used the A3 paper, Sir." Huma said breathlessly. Her pussy was on fire already and the fear she had earlier about begging him to fuck her, she was getting very close to that point.

"And the original was?" He kissed on her shoulder blade, his hot lips pressing to her soft, smooth skin and setting it ablaze.

"Mmmm," Huma could not control the moan this time "It was A4, Sir."

"Which is much smaller…isn't it, doll?" He kissed the side of her neck this time.

Huma felt a hot chill go down her spine "Mmm, yes, Sir." She could feel his dick hard, and thick pressing right between her ass cheeks and it was taking all her willpower to stop from pulling up her dress and begging him to enter her.

"And then again, this one, same mistake?" He kept her squeezed against him as he pointed to the other copy. While he was pointing with the left hand, his right hand was gently caressing her. Huma could feel the warmth of his hand on her skin through the thin dress and was hoping his hand move up from her belly to her breasts which were aching for some attention right now.

"Yes, Sir." Huma said, trying to not let her voice come out raspy and hoarse but failing. Her whole body was charged like she had electric current flowing through her body.

"Do you make such mistakes often, pet?" This time, Vikas did move his hand up, and squeezed her breast in his strong, large hand. Huma wanted to cry out with relief.

"When I am distracted, Sir." She was shamelessly grinding her ass on his cock now, openly inviting him to fuck her right there and then.

"You get distracted easily?" He kneaded her breast as he kissed her neck, just below her jaw line. Her pussy throbbed at the touch of his lips on her skin.

"Only when…mmmm," She moaned as he moved his hand to the other breast and kneaded it even harder "only when you are here, Sir." She blurted it out without thinking. It's not like he didn't already know that she was his for the taking. If she could smell her leaking pussy then he definitely could smell it as well.

"In my office, you would get a spanking until your ass was red for something like this, honey." He was boldly playing with her hot body and Huma never wanted him to stop. Her eyes were half-closed and she couldn't even think about anyone else. It was like she had forgotten that she was in office.

"What a shame that I am not in your office, Sir." Huma said, pressing her butt harder on his dick "A lesson from time to time is good for a girl."

She couldn't believe what she was saying. It was true that she loved being spanked. It was hard for her to find men who could really take charge and be manly without being cruel. This problem she had in common with her boss. But this was not the kind of thing to be shared with a client. Was he really a client in this moment though? Right now his hard cock was grinding on Huma's ass, humping her through the clothes while his hand squeezed and kneaded her hot, heavy tits.

"You should come to my office some time." He said, kissing slowly below her ear.

"Any time, Sir." She said "Whenever you want."

He kissed her neck again before gently stepping back. Huma placed both hands on the copy machine and panted like a dog. Her pussy juices were flowing down her thighs.

Vikas walked back to Shilpa's office door and peeked in.

"Shilpa, when you send me the estimates for the new work, make sure you get Huma to deliver them."

"I was just going to email them to you, Sir." Shilpa said.

Vikas said patiently "Oh, it's so noisy here, I think you didn't hear me. I said when you send me the estimates, get Huma to bring them to my office."

"Yes, Sir. Of course, Sir." Shilpa said quickly.

"Good girl." He closed the door and stepped back.

Huma was standing by her desk. He walked up to her and said "Have you soon, in my office?"

She nodded "Yes, Sir. Looking forward to it."

Vikas reached up easily, hooked his fingers behind her neck and pulled her face closer. Tilting his head he pressed his lips on hers and kissed her slowly but firmly. Huma responded by pressing herself against him and wrapping her arms around his neck. She opened her lips as he took her bottom lip between his lips. Her eyes were closed and she was completely immersed in the hot, wet kiss. She felt his tongue enter between her lips and eagerly pressed closer, parting her lips wider for him. As his tongue explored her hot mouth, she pressed her tits on his chest, feeling her body temperature rise again quickly. His breath mingled with hers in a heady, erotic blend and Huma felt like she was intoxicated.

He stepped back gently breaking the kiss and Huma reluctantly unwrapped her arms from his neck. He cupped her cheek and said "Bye for now, pet."

"Bye, Sir." Huma breathed.

She looked at the closed door of Shilpa's private office then went to the toilet and fingered herself until her pussy exploded on her hand. The whole time, she was reliving every second of the encounter with Vikas. It was mixed with the anticipation of what would happen when she went to his office with the documents.

Chapter 35 – Shilpa Tells Raj the Plan

"You fucked him, didn't you?" Raj Kundra said.

"He is a client, Raj." Shilpa said "It's my job to keep the client happy."

"Is that what you call it, client relations?"

"Well, what do you want to call it?"

Raj said "I think you like him."

"He has a dick that thick and long like a nightstick, you won't find a single woman in the world who would not like him."

This was Raj's kryptonite, he had no reply when Shilpa came right out and talked about penis size.

He sulked for a minute then said "At least could you not fuck him in the office."

"You think I had a choice? I have wanted him for a long time." Shilpa said frankly "This is the first time he responded. I have been hungry for months. When a man like that shows interest in me, I can't say no, he knew he had me and I was not going to lose the chance by saying, please not now."

"But Shilpa," Raj protested "The sounds were all over the office. Your secretary could hear you."

"You think she doesn't want him?" Shilpa challenged "I have seen how she looks at him and bats her eyelashes. She would bend over her desk for him just as easily as I did on mine."

Her graphic description of the fucking position made Raj's dick pulse in his pants.

"But, Shilpa –"

"It's a shame you are being like this," Shilpa interrupted him "I was going to make you an offer."

"Offer? What offer?" Raj perked up.

Shilpa controlled all physical contact in their marriage and "offer" was usually her codeword for when she was going to allow Raj something sexual. He jumped at it like a dog jumps for a biscuit which was her intention to begin with.

"Never mind. I don't think you are interested." Shilpa said "Let's just go to lunch."

Raj said quickly "No, no, I am interested. I am interested. What's the offer?"

Before Shilpa could answer the door opened a little and Vikas peeked in. He wanted Shilpa to send Huma to his office with some documents. When Shilpa said she was going to send them by email, Vikas simply repeated his demand. Raj saw a rare sight that he had not seen before. He saw Shilpa give in and comply like a pet bitch. She said "Yes, Sir." and that guy had the audacity to say "Good girl." in that patronising tone right in front of him, her husband.

"Lucky bitch." Shilpa said "She finally gets what she has been craving."

"You think he will fuck her, too?" Raj asked with a shock, even though he knew the answer. But he found it incredible that this man was asking Shilpa to send another girl to him. He had just fucked Shilpa and now he was asking her to send her secretary to him! Why, the gall of that man!

"What will you do?" He asked.

"I will send her, of course." Shilpa said "I am just glad he is only asking to send her for a visit and not to keep. If he wanted to have her in his office, he would just have to snap his fingers and she would follow him like a pet bitch."

Raj had often checked out Huma and thought she was hot. Of course, he could not make a move or even flirt with her because she was his wife's secretary. He had noticed that she always dressed nice and sexy but sometimes her dresses were more bold and even slutty. Now he was realising those were the days when Vikas came over for a meeting. He thought about Vikas and how rough he would be on Huma like he had used Shilpa just now in her own office.

"So shall we go to lunch?" Shilpa said, bringing Raj out of his reverie.

"No, no, baby, what's your offer, please?" Raj was sure she was teasing him but he was not in a position to call her bluff.

"Well, my pussy has been used and abused hard" Shilpa said, parting her gown and showing him her reddened pussy, messy with cum "I was going to give you a chance to lick it clean and give it some TLC with your tongue."

"Oh yes, please, I want to take that offer." Raj said quickly before she could change her mind.

"You don't mind that my cunt juices are mixed with his cum, do you?" Shilpa said, getting up.

"He came in you?" Raj asked with a shock. She had never, ever allowed him to cum in her.

"Well, it's ok, you don't have to do it if you object to it." Shilpa sat down again.

"No, no, baby, I was just curious. I an not objecting." Raj pleaded "Just curious."

"Ok, then, yes, he came in my cunt, and also wiped his dick on my tits." Shilpa said casually "I had thought of giving you the offer to lick my tits clean too, but you lost that when you bitched about him fucking me."

"Sorry, baby, so sorry. I didn't mean to bitch." Raj folded his hands "I want that offer too, please. I love your tits, you know that."

"We'll see." Shilpa said walking around her desk and to the sofa "Let's see how you do on the first offer."

As she sat down on the sofa, she pulled her gown up around her waist so her legs and pussy were fully bare. She placed one foot on the coffee table and opened her legs wide. Raj walked up between her legs, knelt down on the rug and smelled her pussy. He placed his hands on her thighs and touched his tongue to her pussy slit.

Yes, that was definitely what he tasted when she had kissed him earlier. He started licking her thighs and pussy. He planned to do such a good job that she would allow him to lick her tits clean as well. He rarely got such good offers, her sexual treats for him were usually much less intimate. Vikas having fucked her was turning out to be good for Raj as well. She was combing his hair with her fingers and soft moans were coming out of her mouth. Both were good signs that he was doing well so far.

"By the way," Shilpa pulled his hair and made her look up at her "I have promised Vikas that he can fuck me any time, anywhere, even if you are with me."

"What?" Raj was getting shock after shock. He knew his wife fucked other men, but they were all casual one-time fucks and she controlled the encounters just as she controlled him. This was the first time, he was hearing that someone else had power over her.

"Yes, that was his condition for giving me his dick," Shilpa explained "that he would fuck me every time he sees me, and I said yes."

"But anywhere? Even in public?" Raj said.

"Anywhere means anywhere, Raj. It's his call. Whenever he meets me, he will decide where he wants to fuck me. I will, of course, eagerly cooperate and I think you will as well. Is that clear?"

Raj nodded "Yes, it's clear, honey."

"Just think of me more as his whore rather than your wife now." Shilpa said cheerfully.

"Yes, dear."

"Now, continue." Shilpa said and relaxed her hold on his hair.

Raj lowered his head between her legs and started licking her pussy again.

Chapter 36 – Hina's Hard Audition

Hina's legs were trembling as she followed Parineeti Chopra to the door to Vikas' private office. She was marvelling at Parineeti's short dress. It looked like she would flash her pussy if she bent over even a little bit. But then, Hina looked at her own dress. God, she didn't remember this dress being this short, or this deep cut. Her breasts seemed like they would fall out of the deep neck dress if she made one little move.

While she was looking down at her boobs, she noticed her shoes further down and that made her feel better. The 8" high stilettos looked amazingly sexy and Hina was walking on them like she was born in them. She stopped all her thoughts as Parineeti opened the door and Hina got her smile ready to greet the big boss.

"Sir, your new bitch is here." Parineeti said. Hina thought that was a bit weird to introduce her like that but at least now she knew where she stood. There was no pretence.

"Good afternoon, Sir." She said entering the office, feeling completely out of her comfort zone.

"Hi Hina, come on in." Vikas said.

Wow. Hina had to admit he was even more handsome than his photos. She really wanted him to like her now.

"Come, bring that chair this side," he told her "sit next to me."

Hina pushed the visitor chair around his desk and near his chair. The door closed behind Parineeti and Hina felt that the sexual tension in the room went sky high suddenly. She sat down in the chair, glad to take the weight off her knees that suddenly seemed to be filled with jelly.

"Na, na, na," Vikas said as she started to cross her legs "you will never cross your legs in front of me."

"But Sir," Hina's cheeks flushed red "I am not wearing any panties."

"That's fine. You will never be allowed panties here." Vikas said casually.

Hina slowly opened her legs. As the cool air of the room hit her pussy, she knew she was fully exposed now. He didn't stare at her pussy but he didn't ignore it either. She could see in his eyes that he was inspecting everything.

Vikas said "How often do you shave your pussy?"

"Um…Sir…" Hina wasn't expecting that kind of question right off the bat. She didn't know if he was trying to put her on the defensive or just wanted to emphasise that she was just fuckmeat for him.

"T…twice a week, Sir." She said with an effort "I like to keep it smooth."

"Do you do Kegel exercises?" He asked and picked up a pencil from his desk.

Hina had found a couple of years ago about the exercises that helped a girl keep her pussy tight and healthy. She used to do them regularly.

"Yes, Sir. Regularly." She said. The way he was playing with that pencil, she was sure he was going to ask her to take it up her cunt and squeeze it with her pussy. God, that would be so demeaning. But if he asked, she would have to do it. It's not like she had any choice here.

But he didn't ask her to take the pencil in her cunt. At least, not yet.

"You are a pretty girl, Hina." Vikas said, but before she could thank him, he continued "Pretty girls are dime a dozen in this city. In this business, pretty girls are just piece of meat. That's what you are, do you understand?"

Hina nodded.

Vikas said again "You are gorgeous but you are just a gorgeous piece of meat."

"I am a piece of meat." Hina repeated, showing him that she understood her place.

She was getting more and more uncomfortable. Her nerves were all over her body now. She wondered what would happen if she just got up and walked away. Well, any chance of her ever becoming a model would be down the drain, that would happen. She stayed.

"Good." He approved "Do you have a boyfriend?"

"Yes, Sir. You have met him – Vansh Chaudhary." She reminded him.

"Oh yes." Vikas shook his head "Better let him go."

Hina was dismayed "I have to break up with him?"

"I won't force you to but…" Vikas leaned in "Look Hina, do you want to be a model?"

"Yes, Sir." Hina said eagerly.

"And you want to be a model in VisCom?"

Hina tried to remember what VisCom was, then remembered that it was the company where Vansh worked, where she was sitting right now.

"Oh very much so, Sir." She said with enthusiasm.

Vikas nodded "Then the company will own your ass, and since I own the company, that means I will own your ass."

He looked right into her eyes as he told her the facts and a cold chill went down Hina's spine.

"Do you understand that, Hina?" He held her in his gaze "Who will owns your ass?"

"You will own my ass, Sir." Hina submitted without a struggle.

"And it's not a figure of speech." Vikas told her "I will literally own your ass. So, if you are not ready for that, then go home and forget about being a model."

For a moment, she thought about doing just that. She would have to dump her loving boyfriend. This boss who sounded quite mean would probably fuck her every day. She would be his fuckmeat. No self-respect, no dignity. Just a whore, trading her body for fame and money. The price of becoming a model was too high. But somehow she could not bring herself to get up out of that chair. She had wanted it too much for too long. Now was her chance. She could see it within her grasp. All she had to do was to give up the idea of having a boyfriend and get used to the idea of having an owner.

It's not like she hadn't thought about it before, getting a break in modelling would definitely mean getting fucked by some powerful men, she knew that. But she hadn't expected to be totally owned like an object and being told to dump her boyfriend in the first interview so directly.

These thoughts went through her head in a second and outwardly she just nodded and said "It would be a pleasure to be owned by you, Sir."

Her answer seemed to please him "Good."

"Let's start your first test." He patted his desk "Bend over."

"What? Just like that?" She was shocked. She had not expected romance but this was too crass for her. She looked at the door again and wondered if she could just walk out.

"You expect an engraved invitation for the casting couch?" He said.

"No, no!" Hina stood up and pushed her chair away. There was still time, she could just walk out and never look back. Vansh was a nice guy. She could be happy with him. Of course, he didn't have a big dick like Mr. Malhotra. She wondered how she knew that but she was sure he had a really big, fat cock, but he was not a nice guy.

"Do we…do we have to do this now?" Hina said "I mean tomorrow….?"

Instead of answering her he grabbed her hair and pushed her down on his desk "I said bend over."

"Ouch!" Hina was no match for his strength. Her choice was made for her. She placed her hands on his desk and bent over low.

Vikas opened his pants and pushed his dick into her tight cunt without caring how much pain it caused in her pussy. Hina's body jerked forward with the pain, but somehow she liked it as well. She gripped the edge of his desk with one hand and placed the other flat on it to keep her place.

Then for the next half an hour Vikas drilled her cunt hard and rough. Hina kept screaming with his forceful thrusts but he didn't give her any choice but to surrender under him. She was surprised that she could cum. She came several times as he fucked her expertly, his massive cock ripping her open and making his her bitch just as Parineeti had predicted. Hina could not bear the brutally deep strokes and collapsed on the desk. He continued to fuck her hard, nailing her into the desk and spanking her ass as he fucked her cunt so deep that it was hurting her whole body with each thrust. Hina came several times until she felt her whole body getting weak from the hard orgasms. She wanted him to cum so that she could get out from this abuse.

When he did cum, he took his cock out and pumped his cum all over her naked body. Wait, when did she took off her dress? But that was the least of her problems, his cum on her naked skin was burning her flesh. She could feel it searing through her skin and eating into her flesh. Thankfully, somebody noticed that and pulled the fire alarm. But the noisy alarm just kept ringing with no fire brigade in evidence. Meanwhile, Vikas' cum was still burning through her body. Hina wished somebody would turn off the alarm. It was just annoying her now. Her body was burning but no fire brigade was coming. She noticed there was an alarm point in the room also. She reached out to turn off the alarm….and almost fell off the bed.

The first thing she did was to check if her body was burning. No, it was fine. The fire alarm was still going on, but it was her alarm clock on the side table. She reached out and turned it off.

She wondered why the dream was so goofy. She totally knew that the boss was going to fuck her either in the interview or soon after. And her boyfriend, ha, that was a laugh. As she moved she felt her thighs wet. She reached down between her legs and found that her pussy was soaking wet. She considered fingering herself to an orgasm and relieving the tension. But then decided against it. Not only would it make her late, she should save it for the boss later.

Hina got out of the bed and smiled at her sexy dream.

Chapter 37 – Neetu Has Lunch with Boss

Neetu was very excited but also quite nervous. While she had had this crush on the CEO for so long, she had never had the guts to do anything real about it. It was only last evening that he had shown interest in her and Neetu had responded boldly. She did feel the heat between them. Afterwards when his personal secretary had told her to dress in a shorter, skimpier dress, Neetu had understood that she had noticed the heat as well.

Of course, Neetu had followed her advice. She was wearing a skintight minidress that left her back bare to the very tip of her ass crack. The halter straps that tied behind her neck were thin strings. The dress was made of thin cotton and had a pattern of wide black and turquoise stripes. Being backless no bra was possible with it, but the dress had support in it for her full breasts. Neetu had tied the strings tightly to push her tits up creating a deep, tight cleavage effect. The hem of the dress was only reaching down to her upper thighs. Her long legs were fully bare and looked amazing. Her shoes were 7" high white stilettos with pointed heels. They had 2" high platforms which made Neetu's ass push up in a very sexy, provocative manner.

She had even followed Parineeti's advice and left her panties at home. Her dark hair was loose and created a good contrast with her fair skin. She had red highlights in her dark hair and she had brushed her hair this morning until it all glimmered in light. Neetu actually worried that if she sat down in the lobby like that in that dress, the house detective might think she was a prostitute. She did look super sexy and not like a boring travel desk executive. But she was a travel desk exec at VisCom and had the business card to prove it. She knew people in the hotel staff, including the manager. She decided to be bold and took off her jacket. But she kept it in her lap. That dress was way too short to cover her pussy in the seated position.

They had talked about lunch and Neetu had not thought about anything else since last night. To have a lunch date with boss, to be alone with him, away from the office, just him and her…she had had very vivid, sexy dreams all night. Even now her pussy throbbed when she thought about them. Actually, her pussy was becoming a problem.

Not wanting to make the boss wait, Neetu had left the office early and got to the hotel at half past eleven. Now she would have to wait for at least half an hour. Her pussy was already moist in anticipation and it was only getting wetter. She was worried she might start leaking before Vikas arrived. She decided to not look at the clock and simply pass the time with her phone. She sat on a sofa facing away from the lobby door. It worked. She got her excitement under control. But then the result was that she didn't see Vikas arrive as he entered from behind her.

Vikas arrived two minutes after twelve and looked for Neetu in the big lobby. He found her easily by looking where the men were staring. He walked to her and said "Hi Neetu, sorry I am late."

At his voice, her excitement shot up like a spike. She put the phone down and got up.
"Hello Sir." She smiled "You are not late."

Slipping his arm around her waist, he pulled her close easily like she was his girlfriend. She stepped into his embrace and put her arms around him. He kissed her slowly on the lips like it was his right to do so. Neetu responded with full submission like she had come here just for this. She pressed her body against him and sucked on his lips. His hands gently caressing up and down over her bare back felt so good that Neetu knew she would only wear backless dresses from now on. His tongue played with hers and Neetu pressed her lips harder against his hot, rough lips. She kept her mouth open for him and drank his saliva. His breath caressing her cheek was warming her skin and her pussy.

It was not a long kiss, but just long enough to set the tone for the meeting. Now, Neetu knew she could think of it as a date rather than a meeting. If she was so interested in boss, then he was also interested in having her. His hand on her lower back was telling her that she was already in his possession. She liked that.

"You look smoking hot, babe." He said as they broke the kiss.

"Oh, thank you so much, Sir." She beamed "I could not dress the boring way when on a date with my boss."

She deliberately used the word to see if he would correct her that it was a meeting not a date. He didn't.

"I am flattered." He smiled, keeping his hand on her back, rubbing slowly "Especially those shoes, wow. I love them."

Neetu's smile got wider "Thank you, Sir. They are my favourite."

"The men are all staring at you," Vikas smiled "they are thinking 'Kyaa maal hai!'"

[What a piece!]

She cuddled up closer to him "They should realise by now that this maal belongs to her boss."

He grinned "They will, I am sure. Is my maal hungry?"

"Yes, Sir." She was hungry but she would have happily foregone lunch if he had wanted to do her first. She was loving the direction this conversation was taking and her excitement was rising with every moment.

"Come, let's go to the restaurant, doll." He kept his arm around her as he led her to the hotel restaurant.

Vikas asked for a table that had upholstered sofa type seats along one side. He guided Neetu to sit on the sofa side and was going to sit across from her but she moved and made space for him.

"You will be more comfortable here, Sir." Neetu said.

He smiled and sat down next to her "Thank you, darling."

Neetu scooted closer again and they chatted in a close, intimate manner.

Vikas said "You do look beautiful, sweetheart."

Leaning in close, Neetu whispered "All for you, boss. Your maal, remember?"

He placed his hand on her bare back and kissed her cheek "That's perfect."

The waitress came to take their order. After they placed the order Vikas said "With these new plans for the US deal going on, I am planning to have you work directly under me."

Neetu smiled "That's wonderful news for me." She placed her hand on his leg and leaned in closer "I have been dying to come under you for a long time."

Vikas leaned in as well and pressed his lips on hers. Neetu kissed him back eagerly, parting her lips for his tongue. His hand caressed down her smooth, bare back feeling her silky skin under his exploring fingers. Neetu arched her back as she invited his tongue to enter her mouth by tilting her head and opening her lips a little more. Vikas pushed his tongue into her mouth and the kiss became more heated and passionate. Neetu moaned and sucked his tongue. Her breath was mixing with Vikas' and she could feel her heart beating faster as she felt his tongue fucking her mouth in and out, like a promise of things to come.

The whole lunch went like this, there was a lot of easy, intimate physical contact and Neetu told him, with words and action, that she was available to him however he wanted, wherever he wanted. When they finished Vikas looked at her and asked if she wanted dessert.

Neetu chewed on her bottom lip and shook her head "I'd rather be dessert, Sir, for you."

Vikas placed his hand on her back, pulled her close and kissed her softly "You are a sweet and spicy dish, for sure."

He paid the bill and said "How about giving me a tour of the hotel, darling?"

"Of course, Sir. It would be my pleasure." Neetu said.

They walked out and Neetu took him around to the front garden first, then walked around the hotel, showing him the car park and what the hotel gave them as corporate clients. She walked close with him, holding his arm. They stayed on the concrete path the whole time as her high heels would not be so good on the grass. She took him around to the back garden and showed him the conservatory.

"We have an option to use that for photoshoots if we want, Sir." Neetu said she pointed to the greenhouse.

"Good." Vikas wrapped his arm around her, still supporting her in walking on those high heels but now his hand was caressing her soft, bare back as they walked side by side.

Once they had walked around outside, Neetu took him inside and showed their café which was open later than the main restaurant.

"Well, models don't usually eat anyway." Vikas said, his fingers playing on Neetu's soft skin.

"Yes, but if you and I came here sometimes," Neetu said and added "for an inspection, we could have snacks there."

"A regular inspection is not a bad idea." Vikas said letting his hand slide down rub her firm, rounded butt "But we could just order room service."

"We can, Sir. If we are staying a few hours." Neetu cuddled up to him as they walked to the lift.

"I think a good inspection takes a couple of hours, at least." Vikas squeezed her soft ass cheek slowly, keeping her in his firm grip "What do you think?"

Neetu nodded "You are my boss, I like everything you say, and do." She pressed the button for the lift.

The lift arrived and they got in. Neetu pressed the button for floor 15.

"Do you have time for a full inspection today, Sir?" Neetu said "I can show you one of the rooms they reserve for us."

"It would be a shame to come all this way and not do a good inspection." He kept his hand on her butt "Even if we may not have time for a detailed one."

"Maybe we could schedule a fully details one later this week," Neetu suggested "today you could just start getting familiar with the property?"

"Yes," Vikas nodded "a quick inspection with some in-depth insights."

Neetu looked at him as she walked down the corridor with him "You can go as in-depth as you want, Sir, my whole afternoon is booked only for you."

"Sounds great." Vikas let his hand rub up and down her smooth back.

Taking a key card from her purse, Neetu unlocked a room and entered ahead of Vikas.

"Please, come in, Sir."

He entered and closed the door, locking it from the inside. Neetu put the key card in the slot made for it that turned the lights on.

As Vikas turned from the door, Neetu walked into his arms and pressed her body tightly against his manly form as she kissed him hard. Vikas squeezed her in his strong arms and sucked her lips, his tongue teasing between her soft lips. Neetu opened her lips and accepted his tongue in her mouth. He squeezed her ass in his hands as they continued to kiss passionately hot.

Vikas pulled open his zip and Neetu spread her legs wider as she felt his hot, bare cock between her legs. She reached down, took it in her hand and guided his cockhead to her pussy hole. Then she wrapped her arms around his neck again and kept sucking his tongue. Vikas pushed up with his hips. Neetu moaned as his thick shaft spread open her tight pussy and penetrated her. She moved her hips to grind her cunt on his meaty shaft. Vikas squeezed her tight ass cheeks and pushed her forward into him. His cock entered deeper into her cunt and Neetu broke the breathless kiss with a yelp.

He continued to push deeper into her with in and out strokes until his cock was buried fully deep in her tight cunt. Neetu's breath was ragged and heavy as she tried to get used to her boss' heavy, massive cock in her tight hole. He pushed forward keeping her impaled on his cock and Neetu walked back taking small steps until she felt the bed behind her. Vikas kept his dick in her as he lowered her slowly backwards to the bed. Neetu reached out with her hands behind her and used them to lower herself fully to the bed.

Once they were on the bed, Vikas pinned her under him and started to drill her hard. Neetu was moaning non-stop as she felt his thick cock taking her and subduing her with force. Her pussy was getting hotter and hotter. She closed her arms around him and pushed her hips, loving the feeling of taking him so deep in like she had never been fucked before.

"Mmmm, god, Sir." She moaned loudly as she came on his cock. Vikas kept his strokes hard and deep, slamming her ass into the bed and it made Neetu's orgasm more intense and hot.

He reached behind her neck and untied her halter strap. Pulling down the front of her skimpy dress and he sucked her tits, his tongue teasing her hot, erect nipples.

"Oh god, baby, you made me wait so long." Neetu mumbled as she pressed his head on her breast "Please fuck me hard. Make me yours. I have been craving to be under you for so long."

Vikas moved his mouth along her bare chest, kissing and sucking her soft, warm skin.
"Now you are under me, darling, and I will keep you under me." He whispered in her ear as he sucked her neck.

"Yes, please, Sir." Neetu whimpered "I always wanted to be under you. Please fuck me, oh god, yes, yes, fuck me hard!"

As he slammed her ass into the bed with his long, hard strokes, Neetu clung to him tightly and sucked his shoulder, his neck, and pressed her cheek to his cheek. Her ass was moving up and down as she tried to fuck herself deeper and deeper with his hard, thick cock that was reaching deep into her body. His chest was grinding on her tits and she was feeling her excitement rise. Her nipples were hard. They rubbed on his shirt and she could feel the blood rushing to them as the rough touch of the cloth stimulated them.

"Oh, baby!" Neetu's back and ass left the bed as she arched her body like a bow and then released with a sharp cry when her pussy exploded with a torrent of cunt juices. She pressed her face in the crook of his neck as he pounded her hard into the bed, taking her fully in his possession with each thrust.

She sucked his neck as her body pulsed with the orgasm rushing through her body like a huge wave on the stormy sea. She could feel his hard, throbbing shaft drilling her deep and it was keeping the storm going inside her. She had tears dripping from her eyes. Her arms were closed tight around his body and she didn't want to let go. He was her anchor in that storm. Her pussy clenched and unclenched around his hard cock. Neetu moaned again as her orgasm started to slowly recede. The feeling of having his huge, hard dick still pumping her was wonderful. She kissed his cheek.

"Mmm, boss, that was so wonderful." She whispered in his ear. The next moment, she gasped again as Vikas increased the force of his thrusts.

His cock started to drill her hard and Neetu again started to get that feeling of intoxication which made her completely helpless under him. Her moans rose in volume as her body got hotter and more sexually charged. His thick cock spreading her tight little pussy open wide was incredibly arousing for Neetu and she clung to him while she tried to delay the storm that was coming back. Vikas changed his body position and his chest crushed her soft tits. Neetu let out a long moan and came again all over his cock.

"Aw, baby!" She kissed his neck, the smell of his masculine body making her pussy throb. He continued to pound her into the bed until, suddenly, his hips jerked and he exploded inside her.

"Mmmm." Neetu moaned as she felt the hot load of his cock flowing into her, burning a path through her cunt and flooding her womb. She could feel its heat spreading through her body and her breath getting stuck in her throat. Her hips jerked as her orgasm reached a new peak. She squeezed his thick, pulsating cock with her pussy and moaned at how good that felt.

"You are right," Vikas said as he tried to catch his breath, his cock still sliding in and out of Neetu's soaking wet cunt "we need to have another inspection this week. A more detailed one. And I think this should be a regular inspection. What do you say?"

Neetu smiled "I say you are the best boss in the world." She leaned up and kissed him.

Chapter 38 – Meeting the Hotel Manager

"Boss," Neetu said a few minutes later as they were both adjusting their clothes "speaking of inspection, you need to check out the assistant manager here. She is such a beauty. I think you should bang her."

"I don't mind checking her out, honey, but might not be possible to bang her," Vikas said "we will be leaving our account here."

"Oh. Why, boss?"

"Look, Neetu, if the US deal goes through we will be having American models coming to India to feature in our projects. We should move to a 5-star hotel for that. Also, I want to increase our reserved rooms from 5 to 10. I want to keep one room out of those for my exclusive use."

Neetu walked over to him and cuddled up against him "Will I get some exclusive use in your exclusive room, Sir?"

He put his arm around her and squeezed her tight "Of course. You are for your boss' use, aren't you?"

She nodded "Oh yes, I like the sound of that. For your exclusive use."

"I don't need exclusive." He said "As you know I am married, so I can't have you restricted to me. Fair is fair."

Neetu shook her head "Doesn't matter. I won't need any thing more as long as I am on your menu. Just snap your fingers when you want."

He squeezed her ass and leaned in to kiss her.

"But boss," Neetu said after they shared a slow, intimate kiss "you can still meet this manager, and bang her before we close our account here."

"You seem to think it's just a matter of picking her up and fucking her." Vikas smiled "Why do you think she would be willing?"

"Because ours is a big account for this hotel," Neetu said "and you are a hunk."

"Thank you, darling, but I can't take advantage of our account any more as we will be closing it, I just told you."

"Yes, but she doesn't have to know that."

Vikas grinned "So, I should become a bad guy just for a nice piece of ass?"

"Um, no need to be such a good guy either, Sir. At least see the piece of ass first."

"Well, we'll go talk to her anyway about the account."

"Please don't tell her right away that we are closing the account?"

Vikas shook his head "No, baby, I don't do business that way."

Neetu sighed "I hope you will change your mind when you see her."

=======

"Look, Mrs. Gautam –" Vikas said.

"Miss Gautam, Sir," She interrupted him "and you can call me Yami. How can I help you, Sir?"

She was indeed as beautiful as Neetu had advertised. Her sharp features had a slight softness to them that made her extremely charming. Beautiful lips and big eyes that joined in her smile were enough to make any man fall in love with her. She was wearing a white tank top that was covered by her formal black jacket. Her black pencil skirt reached only half-way to her knees and would have been called a mini skirt if it were a couple more inches shorter. Her long legs were bare and her feet were encased in 5" high heels.

Vikas had checked her out in first glance as he entered and she had welcomed him with an open smile.

"Look, Miss Gautam, Yami," He tried again "not to cast any aspersions on your capabilities, but I would like to see the manager, please. Where is Mr. Talsania?"

"Sir, Mr. Talsania is on a one-month holiday." Yami said "He will be back in three weeks."

"Hmm. So, who is taking care of business in his absence?" Vikas asked.

"I am, Sir!" Yami chirped "I am the assistant manager. What can I do for you, Sir?"

"Ah. I see." Vikas leaned forward in his chair "Yami, the thing is, I am planning to close the account with your hotel. I came to ask Talsania how much notice you would need."

"No, no no!" Yami was out of her chair like a shot "No, no, no, no, no! Closing, no, why, has anything happened, Sir? Any problem with the service? No, that's not good. Give us a chance, Sir. Any problem, you tell me. I will take care of it."

"It's not that, Miss Gautam." Vikas said calmly "There's no problem with the service or the facilities. It's simply a business decision. Our company is growing and we will soon be expecting international guests to travel here to work with us. For that reason, I am planning to move us to a 5-star hotel."

"But Sir, there's not much difference in a five-star from us." Yami pulled a chair and sat next to him. Vikas turned his chair to face her. Neetu simply watched from her seat.

"Sir, a five-star hotel simply has a bigger lobby and better marble, that's all." Yami said earnestly "Our service has a more personal touch which they can't provide. Sir, our service will suit your clients much better, I can assure you."

"I am afraid, Miss Gautam, my decision has been…"

"No!" Yami interrupted him "Don't make the decision yet, Mr. Malhotra. One chance. Give me one chance. I will put together a proposal that will prove to you that we can serve you better. I will tailor everything to your needs. Will you give me one chance, Sir?" She looked into his eyes with a beseeching look.

Vikas looked at Neetu.

Neetu said "Sir, it's not an urgent decision. If Yami thinks she can convince you to change your decision, there's no harm in listening to her proposal. She's not asking you to commit to anything, just asking for a chance to present her side. It's your choice, Sir, but I think she deserves a chance."

Yami gave Neetu a grateful glance.

"Alright, Yami." Vikas said "You have your chance to create a proposal to convince me that my decision to shift to a five-star hotel is wrong. And here's the important bit. If you convince me, we will be expanding our involvement from 5 rooms to 10 rooms, and one of those will be permanently allocated to myself. So, whatever quotation you prepare, make it with those figures in mind."

"Wow, that's great, Sir. Thank you, thank you so much." She put her hand on his arm "I really appreciate this. I have just taken over this job for a week. You are one of our biggest clients. If I lose you, I can kiss my job goodbye. Thank you for giving me a chance, Sir."

"No problem, Yami." Vikas said "Please call my secretary for an appointment when you are ready with your proposal and I will come over for your demo."

"Yes, Sir. I will revert to you within two days." Yami nodded "Thank you so much for trusting me."

Vikas nodded.

Neetu followed him outside.

"What did you think, Sir?" Neetu asked in the car.

"She's a nice piece." Vikas agreed.

"I told you." Neetu grinned "I think you should come alone to see her proposal. I mean if you want to claim her."

Vikas turned to look at her and grinned "Any proposal she puts together has to include her for me to even consider it."

Neetu nodded "I think she's smart enough to realise that."

"We'll find out, won't we?" Vikas smiled.

Chapter 39 – Pooja Hegde Gets the Good News

 "You wanted to see me, ma'am?" Pooja Hegde entered Shilpa Shetty's private cabin.

"Pooja, yes, yes, come in." Shilpa said "Take a seat."

Shilpa waited for the younger girl to sit down while she talked to her secretary "Huma, file these and get the quotation templates."

While Huma went to the filing cabinet near the other wall, Shilpa addressed Pooja.

"I have good news and bad news." Shilpa said.

"Bad news, what bad news?" Pooja looked alarmed.

"The bad news is that I will probably have to let you go." Shilpa said.

"Let me…let me go?" Pooja sat up in her chair "But…but why…like fire me? But why? I thought the presentation went well?"

"It went too well." Shilpa said.

"Too well? I don't understand."

For the first time, Shilpa smiled "That's the good news. Vikas is interested in you."

"Mr. Malhotra?" Pooja perked up "Really, ma'am?"

"Yes." Shilpa nodded "He liked your presentation, he liked your style and I think I can say that he liked you."

"Wow!" Pooja smiled wide "What does that mean really?"

"It means he wants you."

"Like…I mean…like…he wants me?" Pooja said "Like for a job, in his company? But I work here. My agreement says I can't work for a client for a year after I leave here."

Shilpa nodded "I know what the agreement says, I drafted it. But Vikas is a special client. What he wants, he gets. And right now he wants you."

"Wow!" Pooaja could not hide her smile "He wants to employ me?"

"At the moment, he has asked me to send you over for an interview. I don't know what the job is, but he was impressed by your work here and he wants to see you. I am sure he has a job for you. You are smart enough to know how to pass that interview, don't you?"

Pooja nodded slowly "He is the boss and…should I dress nice?"

Shilpa nodded "If you want to pass the interview, you need to dress as he likes."

"Do you know how he likes his girls to dress, ma'am?"

"I sure do. He likes them in tight, skimpy dresses, backless style is his favourite and short dresses with the legs showing will make you his favourite. And he doesn't allow panties."

"Umm, ok." Pooja said.

Huma was taking her time at the filing cabinet as she didn't want to miss a word of this conversation. She made a mental note of Vikas' dress code and filed it away.

Shilpa said "Make no mistake Pooja, if he takes you, he will take all of you. I will have to release you if he wants you, even I can't say no to him when he wants something. But you need to make the choice for yourself, if he offers you a job that means you will belong to him. To put it very crudely, if he wants to bend you over his desk, you will bend over on his command. If he wants you on your knees between his legs, you will kneel between his legs and suck his dick while he works.”

Pooja swallowed once and said “Yes, ma’am.”

“On the other hand,” Shilpa continued “if you don’t want to go, I can tell him that you are not interested. That much I can do, and you can keep working here. If you don’t pass the interview then also you can come back and keep doing your job here. But if he selects you and you accept, then you are his property the moment you sign that employ agreement.”

“What’s the job, ma’am?” Pooja asked “Is it his personal secretary?”

“I don’t know, but I don’t think so. He already has a personal. I have met her several times in meetings and she does belongs to him totally as well. It won’t matter what the job is. If he picked you up personally then you should be aware that you won’t be just his employee, you will be his possession. He will use you any way he likes. It’s your choice to go for the interview or not, but after that…well, Vikas is very dominant and you are a pretty girl, there is not one chance in a million that he will only have you as his employ and not own your ass. As I say, it’s your choice to go or not go.”

“He…he is awfully good-looking, ma’am.” Pooja admitted.

“Oh, he’s a handsome devil. And he knows it.” Shilpa said “I told you he has a personal secretary that he owns. The way she looks at him, I can give you in writing that she loves being his property. He just got married to a stunning girl. But that would not stop him from doing her regularly. I don’t know how many others he has. If he selects you, you will be just one of his bitches. I am sure any girl in this office would be happy if they got the chance you have. But I couldn’t just send you over there without warning you what you will be signing up for.”

“Thank you, ma’am. I really appreciate that.” Pooja said “I…I..I know you are looking out for me, but I think I should go for the interview and do my best. And if Mr. Malhotra wants to take possession…I mean, take me under his control, then I will submit happily. I am sure he is a good boss."

"Oh, you would be a stupid fool to not try your luck." Shilpa said "I just wanted to spell it out for you. He can always find a new bitch for his office, you would never get another chance like this."

"Yes, ma'am. You are right." Pooja nodded "I would like to go for the interview."

"Smart choice." Shilpa said and placed a card in front of Pooja "This is his secretary's number. Call her and ask for an appointment. He said he would like to have you sooner rather than later. He'll be going to US within a month and he would want to train you before he leaves."

"It sounds amazing, ma'am." Pooja picked up the card "Thank you so much for letting me try this."

"As I said, honey, when Vikas Malhotra wants something, there's no girl on earth who can say no to him. Myself included."

Pooja smiled a cheeky smile "I don't plan to say no, ma'am."

"Smart girl. Oh, and Pooja," Shilpa said "wear the highest heels you have. He likes those."

"Yes, ma'am. Thank you." Pooja said.

Huma brought the files over to Shilpa.

Chapter 40 – Hina Meets Parineeti

Hina could not control the butterflies in her stomach as she walked up to the building bearing the name VisCom in large letters. She walked in and took off her jacket before approaching the reception. She had come here before a couple of times and had been turned away from this same reception. She had been told that they only recruited models via the modelling agency and never directly. Her heart was beating fast as she walked up to the same counter again and told the girl behind the computer that she had an appointment. To her relief, she found that her name was in the visitor list and she was told to go up to the 37th floor.

She looked at her reflection in the lift doors. She looked like a model, she thought. Her shoulder length hair were loose around her neck. She had gone bold and allowed her hairstylist to colour it dark brown. It was on a whim but she felt that it looked good. Then she wondered.

Based on Vansh's information she had put on her yellow dress. It had a ring around her neck, and two pairs of double straps leading from the ring to her breasts. There was a nice, deep cleavage as the thin yellow fabric draped over her firm breasts. There was no back to it at all so she could not wear a bra. The dress clung tightly to her butt and squeezed her ass cheeks together. The hem came over the upper thighs but did not cover anything below that. She had left her long, shapely legs bare and chosen 6" high, white stiletto heels with a 1" platform. She was wearing her tiniest yellow thong and it was a good thing that she decided to wear panties because she could feel herself getting very moist as the lift moved up towards the CEO's office.

A look at her watch told her she was arriving 15 minutes early, but she was ok with that. She didn't want to be late and she would be happy to wait for the boss to see her. Hina knew very well where she stood. It was him who could change her life, not the other way round. She would wait all day for him if that's what it took.

"Hi, I am Hina Khan." Hina told Vikas' personal secretary "I have an appointment with Mr. Malhotra."

"Oh yes, Hi! I know." Parineeti said "I am Parineeti. I am his personal. He is not back yet from the field but he should be back soon. Would you like to wait?"

"Yes, please." Hina walked in and took a seat in Parineeti's little office.

Parineeti said "You are a model, right?"

Hina nodded "Well, I am trying. I haven't done anything yet."

"That's ok. Have to start somewhere."

"I tried here before too," Hina confided in Parineeti "but I was told that you don't recruit models directly only through agencies."

"Yes." Parineeti nodded "Usually all our models come via the Kansal agency."

"I gave my CV there, but I never got anything back." Hina said.

"They get a lot of models and frankly, I don't think they pick the hottest ones. I mean you look stunning."

"Oh thank you." Hina smiled "I am hoping…I am hoping…that Mr. Malhotra likes me. I hope he doesn't say go apply at Kansal's."

"No, no," Parineeti assured her "boss can make his own decisions. If he likes you, he will just..." she looked into her eyes "…take you."

"That would be great." Hina said "I am just terrified that he would tell me we don't recruit models directly."

"He is the boss, he can make an exception. He has all the power." Parineeti told her.

"I just hope he likes me enough to make the exception." Hina said, still nervous.

"Of course, he will. Come on, don't you have a mirror?" Parineeti said "Look at you, you are a beautiful piece. And my boss, likes beautiful pieces." She smiled.

"Thank you, Parineeti, you are making me feel better." Hina smiled back "I am even getting in to see him because of my boyfriend."

"You have a boyfriend?"

Hina nodded "He works here, in IT. Vansh Chaudhary."

"Serious?" Parineeti said "Sorry if I am being nosey."

"No, no, it's ok." Hina said "I feel like I can talk to you openly. You are the closest person to Mr. Malhotra, and it's crucial for me to make a good impression on him. And no, it's not very serious from my side, but Vansh, I don't know, I think he might be more serious."

Parineeti appeared thoughtful "It's good that you can be frank with me, and you are right, I can give you the best advice when it comes to Boss. The reason I asked about your relationship…" She paused a moment then continued "Look, if boss makes an exception and hires you directly, it will be for one reason only, that he likes you, personally. If he likes you personally, then…"

"He will want to have me personally, right?" Hina said "It makes sense."

"I didn't want to be crude…"

"No, no, please…be frank with me. I am a model, well, wannabe model, and I am not shy with men. Please tell me honestly what I should do."

"I am guessing boss has seen your photos, right?"

"Yes, of course. Vansh showed him." Hina nodded.

"Then he called you because he thought you were a nice thing." Parineeti said "And as I said he likes to possess nice things."

Again, Hina nodded "Yes, that makes perfect sense. Will I need to break up with my boyfriend?"

"I can't say that. That might be extreme." Parineeti said "But, it's more a question of priorities."

"Of course, boss will be the first priority in my life." Hina said "I am pretty but I am not stupid. I have no doubt that I will need to leave myself in boss' control if I am lucky enough to be his choice."

"Exactly! That's the important part, whether you break up with your boyfriend or not…boss won't even ask you to break up."

"He might not but I have to think about it, no?" Hina said "If Mr. Malhotra selects me that means he will be building my career. I am sure he will need full access to me."

"Absolutely right!" Parineeti agreed "And speaking of access, you are fully accessible, right?" She looked down at Hina's crotch and she got her meaning.

"Umm…just a little thong. Very tiny." Hina said in almost a whisper.

Parineeti just shook her head.

Hina nodded. She stood up, stepped away from the chair and reached up under her short dress. She pulled down her little thong and took support on the chair to pull it over her high heels.

She said "High heels are good until you need to do this." She put the panties in her purse.

"Just stop wearing them completely." Parineeti advised.

"What, high heels?" Hina looked surprised.

"No, no, panties. Boss doesn't like panties." Parineeti corrected "High heels he loves. In fact, you should wear higher, 8 or 9 inch heels with higher platform."

"Oh, wow. Sure. I will buy some." Hina promised "And I will stop wearing panties. It's important to me that my boss has access to me at all times."

"Exactly. Same with me."

"Do you…you think he will do me…in his office?" Hina nodded towards the door to Vikas' private office.

"It's his choice. You just need to be ready, when you walk in that door, you should be completely under his control. That's how you should think about it."

"You are right." Hina said "I don't know why I asked. He is the boss. I have come to him to realise my dream. I should be willing and ready to let him take control of me. I am just so nervous. This can change my life, you know."

"Not can," Parineeti corrected her "it will! I have complete confidence that he will like you."

"Oh, you are so sweet. You really think so?" Hina placed her hand on Parineeti's arm "I mean, you are not just being nice, are you? You think I have a shot?"

Parineeti smiled "You do. A very strong chance. You are beautiful, you are dressed to kill, and most importantly, you are going in with an attitude of complete submission. My boss likes that."

"Complete submission. That's the perfect way to put it." Hina said "I must remember that."

"It's not the words, honey." Parineeti laughed "It's the attitude, and you already have that."

"Thank you, Parineeti, I really appreciate this. I am so glad I came in early. This has helped me a great deal."

"You can call me, Pari." Parineeti smiled "We will probably be working together soon."

Hina smiled "Thank you, Pari."

Chapter 41 – Shilpa is Smug

Shamita entered already speaking "Di, what is this, you didn't even tell me you had a meeting with him today?"

"But you had your parlour, kiddo." Shilpa said in a teasing tone. She was very pleased with herself.

"I would have cancelled the parlour appointment if you had told me about the meeting." Shamita said and took a seat across from her sister.

Shilpa said "I did tell you. I told you we have a client meeting this morning and what did you say? You said you have an important parlour appointment."

"Arre, di! But you didn't tell me the meeting was with him, that the client was Vikas Malhotra of VisCom."

"Why should I?" Shilpa challenged.

"Because you know I have a big crush on him," Shamita wailed "I have been trying to get with him for months!"

"You are not the only one." Shilpa reminded her "Every girl in this office has a crush on him."

"But every girl doesn't have a chance. Today could have been my chance."

"No, today was my chance, you will have to wait your turn." Shilpa said with a smug smile.

"Your chance? You mean? No way! Do you really mean…no, I don't believe you."

Shamita sputtered on like a leaky faucet while Shilpa sat in her with the smug smile getting more smug by the second.

"Really, di?" Shamita said with her eyes wider open. Shamita was a lovely beauty, similar but different from Shilpa. She was a couple of inches shorter than Shilpa, but had the same slender figure with an extremely cute squarish face.

"Mhmmm." Shilpa said, enjoying her sister's confusion and jealousy. This was almost as delicious for her as the actual sex with Vikas.

"You really mean…no, what do you mean? Are you pulling my leg?"

"No, babydoll, I am not. It really happened. Right after the meeting, right here in my office."

"I don't believe you. What happened? I want you to say it, and uncross your fingers."

Shilpa held up her hands "He bent me over this desk and drilled me like I was some cheap whore he had ordered off the internet."

"No way!" Shamita's small mouth opened wide "He really did you?"

"He didn't do me. He used me. He pounded me like a drum. And the sounds that were coming out of my mouth…go ask Huma, I bet she heard them all, and half the office heard them. Oh yes, your jiju was sitting outside, he heard everything, too."

"Oh my God! I am so jealous of you right now." Shamita said "I want to know everything. Tell me everything. Is he big? I bet he's big."

"Shammy, he's huge! I was cursing my kegel exercises that keep my pussy so tight because he was smashing my cunt like…like…like a steel piston jammed up your hole. And then it throbs. Oh my god, Shammy, I am surprised, I wasn't cumming the whole time."

"God, that's hot. But you did cum…not like jiju?"

"He was nothing like your jiju, Shammy." Shilpa said "I came so many times. But he made me ask permission, made me beg for it."

"You? Beg? That's a new one. Usually you make men beg." Shamita said.

"What can I tell you, Shammy, he treated me like I was his bitch, and I responded like I was his bitch."

"How did you even get him to do you, I mean to use you? In the past he's flirted with you a lot but never actually fucked you." Shamita asked. She was squeezing her thighs together as she spoke.

"Oh, our employee gets the credit for that. Pooja Hegde did the presentation and Vikas said later that he wanted her. I put a condition that he had to fuck me if he wanted me to let go of her." Shilpa smiled "He was happy to take the deal."

"Wow! Tell me everything!" Shamita got comfortable in her chair "All the details."

"Don't you want to keep them for later, this evening?"

"Nope, I can't hold off that long, sis." Shamita shook her head "I need to know now."

"Alright, well, as I you can see, I chose my dress carefully." Shilpa indicated her deep neck silver dress which had a high slit right up to her right thigh joint "And I whispered to him in the meeting that I was not wearing panties."

"You did not!"

"Mhmm. I did too." Shilpa grinned.

"Then? Then?"

"While Pooja was presenting, he took advantage of the dark and put his hand on my thigh."

A high-pitched squeak leaked from Shamita's pursed lips.

"Of course, I opened my legs." Shilpa carried "I wanted anything he could give me. I didn't know about the Pooja angle by then."

Shamita nodded and Shilpa continued "So, as Pooja was presenting, he was playing with my pussy."

"Really?" Shamita's mouth opened wide "With everybody right there?"

"Mhmm. He is very bold. He rubbed my pussy and pushed his fingertip into my hole."

"Oh god!"

"Shammy, I wanted to climb up on the conference table and spread my legs for him." Shilpa said "And if he had given me one signal, I would have done just that. I was that hot."

"I bet."

"My pussy was literally leaking. He had me hungry for him just by his touch." Shilpa said "Thankfully, the presentation was short or I would have cum right there and then with a scream."

"Then? After the meeting?"

"I brought him here to flirt some more like always. He had never touched me like that before so I was hoping we would do more than flirt, But then he asked about Pooja and I saw my chance."

"That was a good deal. So smart of you." Shamita was rubbing her thighs together as they chatted, her pussy was quite wet and itching inside.

"He didn't accept it right away. He made me agree that he could fuck me any time, anywhere we met."

"Even in front of jiju?"

"Oh, he doesn't care if I am with my husband, he would just bang me anywhere we meet."

"God. And you agreed?"

"Did I have a choice? Shilpa challenged.

"No, you didn't, I think." Shamita agreed "Then what?"

"Then he fucked me like I have never been fucked in my life. He pounded me so hard, my whole body is sore. I can't walk without moaning."

Another high-pitched squeak came out of Shamita's closed mouth.

"Shammy, that big dick is amazing, but really it's how he uses it to dominate and own a girl that matters." Shilpa was breathing heavy as she thought about that session with Vikas "I mean, I know deep in my bones that any time, anywhere if he said to me 'Shilpa, mujhe teri leni hai.' I will just say 'Yes, Sir.' and spread my legs."

"Fuck!" Shamita breathed "And you came many times you said?"

"Yes." Shilpa nodded "My pussy was in his control. He made me cum whenever he wanted. I think he has some superpower. If he looked at you, I bet he could make you cum with a look."

"Oh, God." Shamita was squeezing her thighs tightly together "Did he cum in you, di?"

"Yes, he did. Oh yes, come here." Shilpa pulled her dress open and offered her tits to Shamita "Smell that."

"Mmmm, that's so hot. What is it?"

"His cum!" Shilpa smiled smugly.

"No way!"

"Yep." Shilpa nodded "He came in me, but after he pumped me full of his hot seed, he pulled out and wiped his dick on my tits like I was his cumrag. My pussy clenched so hard."

"That's so fucking badass to mark someone else's wife like that!" Shamita said.

"He marked me inside and out. His cum felt like it was burning its way through my cunt into my womb."

"Mmmm. But di, you are on the pill, right?"

"I am, but if I knew he was going to fuck me today, I would have stopped taking the pill."

"Di! What are you saying?"

"Shammy, if he pumped me full of his seed and I got pregnant, I would not mind raising his child."

"Oh my god. What will you tell jiju?"

"I will tell him the truth."

"You will?"

"Mhmm." Shilpa said "Raj already know I am Vikas' whore now."

"How?"

"I told you he was sitting outside when Vikas was banging me into the desk. Then later I told him about Vikas' deal that he can fuck me any time anywhere."

"Did he accept it?"

"Of course. Did he have a choice?"

"Di, please, when will you introduce me to Vikas?"

"You have met him many times in meetings, Shammy."

"No, not like that, di." Shamita shook her head "More like 'This is my sister Shamita, I am sure you will enjoy fucking her'. Like that."

Shilpa laughed "I might not use those words but I will tell him you are interested."

"When?"

"In the next meeting." Shilpa said "Wear a very short dress, skin tight. He likes those. And no panties."

"Ok." Shamita nodded "When is the next meeting with him?"

"Next week some day."

"God, I have to wait a week?" Shamita groaned.

"Why so impatient, Shammy? You have been waiting all this time.

"Di, I had sex with Rohit last night."

"Having sex with your husband makes you want to fuck around?"

Shamita nodded "If I don't have any sex for a while, it's better, but if I let him fuck me then I crave some real sex after that very badly."

"I understand. I have the same problem." Shilpa nodded "Don't worry. He has asked for new quotes for expansion. I will get those papers ready soon and arrange the next meeting."

"Can I take the papers to his office?" Shamita offered.

"No," Shilpa shook her head "he has asked me to send Huma."

"Huma, your secretary? Is he going to fuck her?"

"I am very sure she won't leave his office unfucked." Shilpa said.

"Oh god, when will I get my chance?"

"You will. Don't worry." Shilpa said "but Shammy, I can only introduce you. It's up to him if he wants to bang you or not."

"I didn't think of that. What if I wear a very, very short dress?"

Shilpa nodded "He seems to like those, and you are a pretty girl. We will plan something. I might invite him for dinner one night. Then he can do both of us."

"Mmmm, that just made my pussy twitch."

"Let's try next week's meeting first, then we will plan for the dinner." Shilpa said.

"Yes, di. We should go out tonight to celebrate."

"Sure." Shilpa said.

After leaving Shilpa's office, Shamita went to her own office. She locked the door and put a lot of tissues under her. Then she fingered herself while thinking about Vikas Malhotra fucking her on her desk. She came hard and soaked the tissues as well as her chair. She collapsed forward on her desk.

It took her a couple of minutes to recover. Then she cleaned everything up and unlocked her door.

Chapter 42 – Hina Meets Vikas

In the end Vikas was only 10 minutes late. Hina was on tenterhooks but she kept her cool with conscious effort.

"Hi Pari, Hi Hina!" He said "I am sorry I got late."

"You know me, Sir?" Hina got up in excitement.

"Silly girl." He grinned "I have seen your photos."

"Oh, right." Hina laughed "Sorry, I am nervous. I forgot about the photos."

"No problem. Give me a minute then, Pari – " He broke off as his phone rang. He took it out of the pocket and said "I need to take this. Come on in."

As Hina started to follow him, Parineeti held her arm and stopped her. She signalled Hina to wait. Vikas went into his office.

Parineeti said "Give him a minute. Fix your dress, check your make up, make sure you are ready for the most important interview of your life."

Hina followed her advice then said "I am ready."

"Let's go." Parineeti took her in tow and pushed through the door that bore the legend "Vikas Malhotra – Private".

Vikas was standing by the far wall which was all glass. The curtains were open so the road traffic could be seen in the distance. But Vikas had his back to the view as he was leaning back on the glass while holding the phone to his ear. Parineeti signalled Hina to stay then, leaving her near the door, she walked in and dropped some papers on Vikas's desk. Then she walked up to him until she was right next to him.

He wrapped his arm around her waist, his hand resting on her hip and pulled her close. She went with his pull. He tilted his head and kissed her full on the lips. He kept the phone slightly away from his ear as he sucked her lips. Hina could see that it was not a casual peck but a full, intimate kiss which indicated that Parineeti was fully his personal. She felt a tingle between her legs as she watched him claim what was his without caring that Hina was watching. Or perhaps she liked it because it showed that he already considered Hina also very much in his possession.

Well, he wasn't wrong, Hina thought. She had already come in prepared to do whatever was needed in order to get her career started. But after seeing what a good looking man her potential boss was, Hina's perspective had changed. Now she really wanted him to take her. Her career was still important but now if he offered her a role without a casting couch, she might request him to fuck her. She saw him move his hand down and squeeze Parineeti's ass before they broke the kiss.

Parineeti got out of his arms and came back. She whispered "Complete submission. Go."

Then she went out. Hina took a few hesitant steps towards Vikas. He saw her and beckoned. She walked up to him then. He put his arm around her and easily pulled her close. Hina went with his hand just as Parineeti had. She felt a chill go up her spine as his hand landed gently on her lower back. The heat of his warm hand on her bare back was more exciting than Hina could have imagined. He gathered her easily in his arm and pulled her close until her body was pressing lightly on his.

"What do you want me to tell Pari?" Vikas said in the phone while he slowly caressed Hina's smooth bare back up and down. She gently pressed herself on him and placed her hand on his chest.

He leaned in and kissed her cheek while he let the other party talk. Hina stayed close and pressed her breasts lightly on his chest through her thin cotton dress.

"And why should I tell her not to talk to your models?" Vikas said, while his fingertips grazed lightly up along Hina's spine. She suppressed a moan.

"She was not your model, by the way. Your agency had rejected her." Vikas spoke in the phone. Hina stayed in his casual embrace. She was pressing on the right side of his chest as the was holding the phone in his left hand. Moving quietly, she opened her legs and placed one high heel behind his foot. She gently pressed close against his thigh. She felt her breath catch in her throat as her pussy rubbed on his leg. It was a good thing he was busy on the phone and didn't see her reaction.

It was her very first meeting with him, but Hina was absolutely loving the way he was casually keeping her intimately close. His hand was caressing her back, boldly moving up and down on her silky smooth skin. Once she thought his hand was going to go down to her ass like he had squeezed Parineeti but he stopped and let it caress on her lower back only. Hina took a chance and kissed softly on her jaw. He turned his face towards her and smiled.

As he leaned in, Hina excitedly turned her face up. He kissed her on the lips, slowly pressing his hot lips on her soft, red lips. Hina's heart was racing. She parted her lips. But he pulled back just then.

"Did you sign a contract with her?" Vikas said in the phone, still keeping Hina in his embrace. She surrendered herself in his casual embrace and tried to control herself. She had the impulse to climb up in his lap and ride his cock while he talked on the phone. Instead she settled for kissing his jaw again, then getting bolder, she kissed his neck, just below the jaw line. He didn't stop her. His smell made her pussy clench.

Vikas repeated "Did you have a contract with her?" His hand moved up and down her bare back in a loving caress "Then she was not your model."

He brought his mouth to her face and squeezed her tighter into him as he kissed her cheek and then her neck. Hina could not suppress a moan this time. She pressed her pussy on his thigh, and pressed closer on his chest until her soft breasts were flattened against his manly form. She could feel her body react very strongly to his nearness, his boldness and his physical presence.

"We hire models from your agency, Rohit, because we find it convenient. We are not bound by it." Vikas continued speaking in the phone. Hina boldly turned her face up and kept it turned up while he talked "We are well within our rights to hire any models from anywhere."

Then he noticed her upturned face and smiled before leaning in. This time he pressed his lips harder on hers and when she parted her lips, he slipped his tongue between them. Hina's pussy twitched as Vikas' tongue moved in over her lower lip and touched her tongue. She pressed harder against his lips and sucked his tongue hungrily. She could hear someone saying "Vikas? Vikas?" in the phone while Vikas slowly fucked her hot mouth in and out with his probing tongue.

"Are you there?" The voice in the phone said and Vikas pulled back gently.

"Of course, I am here." He said. Hina tried to control her breathing. Even the brief but intimate kiss had left her highly excited. She could feel her pussy flooding with juices. She clung to him more intimately, the boundaries in her mind about this being an office situation were blurring. She was feeling more like she had been on a date with him and the dinner had gone well. Now they were at his place and they both knew how the night was going to go.

His fingers still lingered on her bare back as he resumed his conversation on the phone "Why would I send her back to you, Rohit? Yes, she had and you rejected her. So, why should I reward you for your bad judgement by paying you commission for finding a model that you didn't actually find?"

Pressing herself against his hard, masculine body, Hina slowly rubbed his chest, her fingers slipping inside his jacket and feeling his pectoral muscles through his shirt. His hand roamed over her back freely and Hina wished he would let it go lower to grab her ass.

"Oh, we are not fighting, Rohit." Vikas said "You would know if you were in a fight with me, because your life would be flashing before your eyes."

In stark contrast to his firm and menacing tone on the phone, his hand on her body was gentle and teasing. Hina bent her knee and pressed her pussy squarely on his thigh. Her dress was thin and she was sure he could feel the warmth of her pussy on his leg, just as she could feel the heat coming from his hard cock that was rubbing on her thigh. Maybe he took her movement as an invitation and his hand dropped lower. His fingers cupped her firm, rounded buttock and squeezed once. Hina pressed her ass into his hand and kissed his neck, encouraging him to explore her further.

She really wanted to have his dick in her right now. She wouldn't have minded sucking his cock while he talked on the phone, but it was her first meeting with him and she didn't want to ruin her chances by doing anything he had not ordered. It didn't stop her from imagining it though. She gently massaged his dick with her warm thigh as they cuddled standing up against the glass.

"Absolutely not, Rohit." Vikas said "That model belongs to me now. She's VisCom property."

Hina had already guessed that he was talking to Rohit Kansal of the Kansal modelling agency. She found it encouraging to observe that Vikas was open to claiming models directly because Hina had also applied to Kansal's after her last visit to VisCom and this same situation might arise about her. She wished he would say about her soon that she was his property too. She knew he said "VisCom property" but he owned VisCom so a girl who was VisCom property was actually his property. Hina wanted that. She wanted it badly.

She continued to listen but her focus was still on staying close to Vikas and encouraging him to explore her further. She felt his hand move down to her butt and she wiggled it a little to tell him he was welcome. He kneaded her tight ass cheeks and kissed her neck softly while he listened to Rohit speak from the other side. Hina turned her head up, giving him full access to her slender neck. She could hear some words spilling out of the phone as Vikas didn't have it pressed to his ear, but by now her focus was going. She could feel her body getting hot and it was becoming harder to think of anything except being in his arms and fully surrendering to him. She wished Rohit would shut up so Vikas could take her and make her his property like she craved.

"Well, Rohit, if you feel that frustrated with it, I am sure I can find a modelling agency who doesn't find me that frustrating." Vikas said and held the phone away from his ear while Rohit sputtered on the line.

This time Vikas pulled Hina right in front of him and hugged her tight as he pressed his lips on hers. She was only too eager to respond. She wrapped her arms around his neck and kissed him back with a passion like she had been waiting for it all her life. She parted her lips as she kissed him, sucking his bottom lip in her mouth. His tongue touched her upper lip and Hina moved her mouth to take it in. She could feel his breath on her face as she sucked his tongue while pressing her tits on his chest. Hina started moaning as Vikas fucked her mouth in and out with his tongue. She could feel his cock getting hard between her legs and suddenly things felt so surreal and excited like she was back in her dream.

He broke the kiss slowly when Rohit started to clamour for attention again from the phone. Vikas put the phone to his ear but kept Hina in his arms.

"Rohit, any time you want to make it real, let me know. Bye." Vikas said and disconnected the call.

"Put it away, please, darling." He handed the phone to Hina and motioned towards his desk. Hina stepped away, reluctant to get out of his embrace but happy that he was off the phone now. She put the phone on his desk and came back to stand in front of him. She was getting that first date feeling again when things are going so hot you know you are going to have sex tonight and it's going to be amazing.

"So, Hina," He took her hands and held them in his hands as he looked into her eyes "you want to be a model."

"If you think I am good enough, Sir." Hina said. She still had the taste of his lips on hers and she wanted more. She wanted to get the work talk out of the way so they could get to the casting couch.

He brushed a strand of hair from her face, his fingers caressing her cheek "You are a beautiful piece for sure."

"Thank you, Sir." Hina said "I was so glad you liked my photos."

"Yes, they were nice. I am glad to see you wore this dress today." He looked down at her sexy, short dress that was displaying her young, stunning body so nicely.

"I asked Vansh which photos you liked, so I wore the one you seemed to like the most."

"Smart girl." He said, cupping her cheek.

"What my boss likes is important to me." Hina said.

"Good. I like that. I was actually surprised to see Vansh didn't take any nudes after that. You looked amazing in that shoot."

Hina smiled "He did Sir. I love posing for nudes. He probably didn't send you those."

"Oh, I see."

"I have a copy of all the photos, Sir." She told him "I will send you those nudes tonight."

"Good, I will wait to see them." Vikas said.

"Not a good idea to make the boss wait for what he wants to see." Hina said and stepped back.

She reached behind her neck and unclasped the metal ring holding her dress straps in place. Then wiggling her hips she worked the dress off her thighs and took it off. She dropped the dress on a chair and stood in front of him, fully naked, her slender, shapely body looking like a million dollars in the office lighting.

"Damn, what a hot bitch you are, Hina." Vikas said. He extended his hand Hina took it. He pulled her closer.

"Thank you, Sir." Hina said "Hot enough to be VisCom property, Sir?"

She moaned as Vikas dipped his head and took her breast in his mouth. His tongue teased her nipple, making her pussy throb in response.

"You want to be VisCom property," Vikas said looking into her eyes as he fondled her soft, warm breast "or my property?"

"Mmmm." Hina shifted her weight, her body was so excited, she could not stand still. She looked in his eyes "Your property, Sir, definitely your property."

He held both her tits in his hands and kneaded them slowly "Are you sure?"

"More than anything, Sir." She pushed her chest forward, pressing her firm, fleshy tits in his hands "If you think I am hot enough to be your bitch."

"Only one way to find out." Vikas said and the simple sentence sent chills down Hina's spine. She had a feeling that thing were about to happen and the anticipation was burning through her body like a wildfire.

He took her hand and led her close to the glass. Under his guidance, Hina placed her hands on the glass and pushed her ass back. She opened her legs wide. Her breath was heavy and she could feel her heart thump in her chest. She heard the sound of his zipper opening and her heart skipped a beat. She expected him to have a big cock and she could see that she was right as soon as he placed his cockhead on her pussy hole. She was soaking wet already and he took advantage of that by pushing his massive, thick rod smoothly deep into her tight cunt.

"Ah, mumma!" Hina screamed as he jammed several inches of his thick, long beast into her tight pussy. Her body shivered with the pain that originated in her cunt and flooded her whole body.

Now she knew how he was going to claim her. Already her legs were shaking with a mix of fear and excitement. His cock was big enough to seriously hurt her. She could feel that raw power already. Hina had come in ready to surrender to him but now she knew that she would not have any other choice. She hoped that he would make her a model, but she knew for sure that he was going to make her his whore.

Vikas moved his hips slowly back and forth. Hina yelped as his movements caused pain waves to shoot up from her pussy like electric shocks. She could see the traffic down on the road and while she didn't know how much anyone could see from outside, she had a distinct feeling of being fucked in front of the whole city. It was like he was showing her that she would belong to him completely even if the whole world were watching. She mewled helplessly. He was right. She was already pushing her ass back without even thinking about it. Her body wanted that cock in her, pain or no pain.

When he ran his hands slowly up along her bare back, Hina moaned uncontrollably. The soft, gentle caresses were controlling her mind as much as the painfully tight fucking from his huge cock. She had no doubt that his cock was going to own her. She had had it in her less than a minute and she could totally understand how helpless she was in front of that cock. It was not just her boss' cock, it was her real owner. Hina was no longer worried about the modelling career, she was hoping he would give her that cock again and again.

"Mumma!" She screamed again as he started to fuck her with long, smooth strokes and she came as soon as she felt his cockhead reaching up into her cunt, controlling and owning her body.

Hina loved sex and had had her share of boyfriends both in J&K and in Bombay. They had always been delighted and sometimes shocked by her appetite for sex and her adventurous spirit. But she could feel that now she had met her match. Mr. Malhotra was the man who could make a girl cum by just asking her the time and here she was in his hands, skewered on his cock and learning her place as his whore. She pushed her ass back, frantically fucking herself on his massive cock as her pussy soaked his big meatpole with her cum. She was panting like a bitch as she pushed back and helped him penetrate her deeper.

"Ah! Ah!" She yelped as his cockhead started to plough into her cervix. That incredibly deep penetration added to her feeling of being completely helpless under his control and while the hot orgasm was masking the pain she could clearly feel that he was incredibly deep inside her.

Not only was his cock fucking her unbelievably deep, it was causing such hot, powerful waves of pleasure in her body that Hina was in an altered state of mind. She had transcended from the real world where she was bent over and taking her potential employer's cock on his glass window to the world where she was Vikas Malhotra's whore and lived to please him. Anything she could do to make him happy was her whore duty to do. Taking his cock in her cunt and letting him drill her like a cheap whore was the least she could do, she must find other ways to make her new owner happy.

Her orgasm subsided gradually but her arousal level did not go down by far. She was feeling like the pot of milk on the stove that is just about boil over and you are blowing on it to keep from overflowing the pot and flooding the whole kitchen. She was that pot, and sexual charge was the boiling milk, any moment it would boil over again and soak her body from inside and outside. She kept whimpering as Vikas fucked her hard and deep. When he moved his hands to her front and took hold of her hot, heavy tits, Hina yelped with an abundance of helplessness.

She knew he was already claiming her and controlling her body but his hands on her soft, sensitive tits would add fuel to the fire and…

"Oh god!" Hina screamed as she came again. His rough, calloused hands on her tits, her sensitive, hardened nipples pressing on his palms had done the trick and sent her body to the overflowing point. She closed her eyes and rode the savage orgasm like one tries to hold on to a wild horse that is as thrilling as it is dangerous.

Clutching the glass with both hands, Hina pushed back hard. She was offering him her pussy. This was all she had to give him in return for the incredible pleasure he was giving and she wanted him to know that it was all his. She pushed back and squeezed his dick with her cunt muscles, hoping to show him that she was a good whore and happy to be in his possession.

"You will belong to me, Hina." He whispered in her ear as he kneaded her soft tits and kept fucking her juicy, wet cunt.

Hina was only too glad to be able to express all that she had been feeling.

"I am your property, Sir." She moaned "Please, please fuck me like your bitch. I am yours, Sir, all yours, completely your whore." She pushed back at the same time to add credibility to her words.

"Yes, you are my whore now, darling." He said amid hard, powerful thrusts of his hips. She was happy that he believed her. His acceptance meant everything to her.

Just then her body jerked again and she cried out as she came again. Her knees buckled and she would have collapsed had she not been so fully skewered on his massive cock. Vikas pushed forward and pressed her body against the glass. Now she had no space to collapse. Her body was pressed firmly on the glass and he was drilling her from behind. Her tits were flattered on the cold glass and he was holding her by the shoulders crushing her against the hard glass with ruthlessly hard and brutally deep strokes.

The feeling of being fucked in front of the whole city intensified and Hina's orgasm went into overdrive. She felt like not just the people in the nearby buildings but the whole population of Bombay city could see that she was being pounded by his cock and now she was Vikas Malhotra's personal whore.

Hina could not help but feel a strong sense of pride as she thought of herself as his whore. She was proud that he had taken her right away without waiting at all to claim her. She was happy and proud that he had considered her good enough to be his whore. She was glad that she had followed his secretary's advice and managed to become his bitch so quickly. The receding orgasm generated hot, electric aftershocks and Hina yelped with each one.

Even as the orgasm was slowing down, her body was still so close to the edge that she expected to burst into another orgasm any moment. This heightened sense of excitement was working on her like a drug. She was feeling no pain from Vikas' fat hard cock drilling her cunt. Every stroke was a powerhouse of pleasure that was flooding her body with such amazingly wonderful sensations that Hina was ready to sign off her soul to the man who was doing this to her. At some level, she knew that his heavy, massive cock was destroying her pussy in a way that would make her sore for probably a week, but she found herself unable to feel anything but gratitude that this cock claiming her.

She had no control over her moans and screams at this point and she was not even thinking who would be able to hear her. From where she was, she felt like the whole city could see her getting fucked on the glass. Everybody knew that Hina Khan was Vikas Malhotra's whore and that's all there was to it. She came again, quickly and suddenly. Her body just jerked against the glass and her pussy overflowed with her cunt juices, soaking her thighs in the oily, sticky fluid gushing from her pussy hole with each stroke of Vikas' cock.

Hina's vision blurred and the lights of the city became fuzzy. She closed her eyes and surrendered to her orgasm.

This one lasted very long, and Hina lost all sensations of her physical body. She became immersed in the pool of pleasure that felt like it was inside her and outside at the same time. Her body was just an ethereal thing flowing through this pool while the pool flowed through her. She was still yelping with Vikas' powerful strokes but she was not aware of it herself. All she was aware of was the incredible pleasure, the immense joy coursing through her very being. Hina loved Yoga and she meditated regularly, but she had never felt the peace and happiness that she felt at this moment. And that's when she really became his property.

"Ah, mumma!" Hina screamed out as she felt a volcano go off so deep inside her cunt that she felt like the burning lava was flooding her whole body all the way to her toenails. She pushed her ass back, happy that she had been able to give her new boss that same pleasure that he had given her.

She continued to squeeze his cock with her pussy, milking his hot seed in her cunt as she mumbled "Thank you. Oh god, thank you so much, Sir. I love your cock. I love being your whore."

"Now you are my property, baby." Vikas kissed the back of her neck. He kneaded her soft, warm tits, his hot breath playing on her neck.

"Thank you, Sir." Hina breathed "I will be a good whore for you, I promise."

"I know you will, darling." Vikas pulled out of her slowly. He turned her around and kissed her lips before guiding her down to her knees.

Hina showed no hesitation in taking his cum-drenched cock in her mouth and sucking it clean. She looked up into his eyes and sucked him slowly but thoroughly. She held on to his thighs and tried to convey to him that she was worshipping his cock with her mouth. Her tongue worked expertly below his shaft, then around it, licking the tip, licking his balls. She worked to get every single drop of his cum from everywhere. She looked down and saw spatters of cum on his shoes. Without a moment's hesitation, she bent over low and licked his shoes clean. She gave them her full attention and made sure that they shone when she finished.

"Good girl." Vikas said and Hina looked up, giving him her sweet, sexy smile.

Chapter 43 – Hina Becomes a Model

A little while later when Parineeti entered Vikas' cabin, Hina was dressed again and sitting in a visitor chair. Vikas was in his seat, his pants properly zipped. But the strong smell of sex was still in the air.

"Sweetie, you started a list yesterday of the models VisCom is selecting directly, didn't you?" Vikas said.

"Yes, Sir." Parineeti said "There's only one name on it."

"Good, put Hina's name on it as well, darling."

"Sure, Sir. Congratulations, Hina."

"Thank you, Pari." Hina smiled wide.

"Sir, can I leave early today?" Parineeti asked "I have some stuff to do at home."

Vikas smiled "It's not early any more, honey. Almost 5 already. Of course you can go. Come and say goodnight when you are ready."

"Thank you, Sir."

She was back in a few minutes "I am leaving now, Sir. I have put Hina's name on the list."

Vikas beckoned her to him. She walked around and he easily guided her to his lap. He put his arms around her and squeezed her as he kissed her on the lips. Parineeti melted in his embrace. She pressed her lips on his and sucked his lips eagerly. He rubbed her back gently up and down as they made out openly, ignoring that Hina was in the room. Parineeti already knew that Hina was now his whore and Vikas knew that Parineeti knew.

The kiss began slow and intimate but soon became passionate and loaded with sexual energy. Parineeti pressed her tits into his chest and took his tongue in her mouth. His hands on her back caressing her up and down, making Parineeti moan with desire. She wrapped her arms around his neck and pressed even closer. She sucked his tongue and swallowed his saliva like she had been hungry for it all day. He pushed his tongue deeper into her mouth, exploring her hot, sweet mouth boldly. They only broke the kiss when both of them were breathless.

"Mmmm, thank you, Sir." Parineeti moaned "I really needed that."

"You are welcome, my love." He cupped her face in his hand and kissed her cheek "I am going to my mother-in-law's tonight, so I might be a bit late in the morning."

"Ok, Sir. May I go now?" Parineeti was still on his lap.

He nodded "See you tomorrow, darling."

"See you tomorrow, Sir." Parineeti slowly got off his lap and left saying bye to Hina on the way.

=========

"Thank you so much, Sir." Hina said "I am so happy you liked my photos."

"You are most welcome, darling." Vikas said "It's my pleasure to have you as a model for our company. Come, I will take you down to the studio. I am not sure but if Shweta is around, I will introduce you. She usually works late."

Shweta Tiwari was around. She was on the studio floor tidying up after a long shoot when Vikas entered followed by Hina.

"I thought the whole reason you hired assistants was so that they could do that kind of chores for you." Vikas said as he walked in.

"These days assistants expect you to assist them." Shweta left the tripod she was folding and came forward to greet her boss "I need to find better ones."

Vikas easily took her in his arms and softly kissed her on the lips. It was not a French kiss, but Shweta turned her face up and pressed her lips back on his.

"Come, meet, Hina Khan, she is a new model with us." Vikas kept his arm around Shweta's waist as he introduced her "I promised you two more models for your campaign, she's the first one. I will find you one more."

"Hi Hina, welcome." Shweta shook hands with Hina "Thank you, Sir. If Rohit were sending us good models, I wouldn't have to bother you with this."

"I don't mind, darling." He caressed her back softly "But yes, Rohit needs to up his game otherwise we'll need to find a different solution."

"Thank you. I am glad you are open to new solutions. I was worried you might stick up for your friend."

"Friendship is good in its place, but I can't let that affect our business." Vikas said "How about Hina though, will she suit your campaign?"

Shweta looked her over "She has a sweet face and a nice body. I am sure she will be fine."

"Thank you, ma'am." Hina said happily.

"Call me Shweta, this is not high school." Shweta grinned. She took out her phone and handed it to Hina "While you are going through contract paperwork I can send you some stuff to read. Give me your email and phone number."

"Ok. Thanks." Hina took the phone.

"What next for her, Shweta?" Vikas said.

"I will do a test shoot with her and confirm that she will suit the campaign, then we'll take it from there." Shweta said.

"Excellent." Vikas said.

"Speaking of test…" Shweta pulled Vikas aside "she seems a bit dazed. Have you been testing her?"

"Just doing my duty as a boss." Vikas grinned "Need to ensure we only take quality pieces."

"Oh, I can't blame you, she is a nice piece," Shweta agreed "and that dress is gorgeous."

"Speaking of gorgeous pieces," Vikas looked down at her "what happened to you? You used to dress like a hottie and suddenly I am seeing you dressed as a construction worker."

That was an unfair analogy on Vikas' part but Shweta was wearing a simple sleeveless top and blue jeans. She looked very cute but nothing like the bombshell she really was.

"Well, I used to dress for my handsome boss," Shweta said "but you never call me and never come down to see me. So, now I dress for these four walls."

"Oh, I see."

"But that stops now, next time, I promise, short dress, lots of cleavage." She smiled into his eyes.

"I like the sound of that." Vikas wrapped his arm around her waist again and kissed her softly.

This was a longer kiss but it was still not much more than a peck on the lips. As he was pulling back though, Shweta put her hand behind his head and pulled him into her. She licked his bottom lip as they continued the kiss. Vikas opened his mouth and Shweta eagerly pushed her tongue into his mouth. Vikas teased her tongue with his and Shweta moaned as the kiss suddenly grew much hotter. She pressed her body against his frame and Vikas wrapped both his arm around her slender, firm body. Their breaths mingled together in an erotic blend. Shweta rubbed his neck, at the base of his hairline and offered him her tongue to suck. He sucked it deep into his mouth while he crushed her soft, warm body against his chest.

Shweta was completely breathless when they broke the long kiss. She didn't try to talk. Instead she walked away to Hina and took her phone back from her.

"It was nice seeing you, darling." Vikas said as he walked up to the two girls. He put his arm around Shweta's waist again but didn't pull her closer "I am going to drop Hina home. I will see you later."

"When?" Shweta said.

"Huh?" Vikas stopped.

Shweta looked at him "When will you see me again, you know, to check the dress?"

"Ummm," Vikas thought for a moment "tomorrow is quite meeting heavy, Friday I have to sort out Kansal, then afternoon,…"

"Vikas!" Shweta looked at him with rebuke.

"Friday." He said "Let's meet on Friday."

"Ok, that's better." Shweta smiled "I will call Pari to fix the time."

"Yes, that's best. She knows it better than I do." Vikas said.

"I know. That girl is so good." Shweta said "She is perfect as your personal."
Vikas was thinking about that as he left with Hina.

Chapter 44 – Hina Gets a Lift

Hina was so glad that Vikas was dropping her home. After her interview with him she was feeling quite exhausted and a bit shell-shocked. She was happy that she would not have to brave the hassles of public transport. But most of all she was happy that she had Vikas' company for a while more. She had loved the whole time with him and didn't want to say bye to him just yet. She knew that he was married so she wasn't looking for any romantic relationship with him, but she was thrilled to be working under him. She expected him to call her to his office and fuck her regularly as was his right as her boss.

In the car, he asked her about herself and she told him about her struggles as well as her current life. He listened to her and asked questions. She shared with him openly, without hiding her current situation or her weaknesses. The only thing she didn't tell him was that she dreamt about him last night.

When they got to her apartment, he pulled over by the side and looked at her.

Vikas said "I am so glad you came in, darling, I am happy to have you."

"I am also happy you had me, Sir." Hina smiled.

He laughed and leaned in "I mean as a model, darling." He cupped her cheek in his hand and smiled "Naughty girl!"

She smiled "I meant the audition, Sir."

"I know that now." Vikas said. He got out of the car and opened Hina's door. She stepped out.

"Work with Shweta." Vikas said "Tell her you are a new model, she will guide you. She's a nice girl."

"Thank you, Sir." Hina was heart was racing, but she said "Sir, do you want to come up and see my apartment?"

"Not tonight, sweetheart." He said "I have to go to my in-laws' I will get late if I stop."

"Oh ok." She opened her arms to hug him and Vikas stepped closer. She wrapped her arms around his neck and kissed him boldly.

It was getting dark now but Hina didn't care who could see her kissing him by the side of the road. She boldly pressed herself into him and sucked his lips. He tasted her lips with his tongue, their breaths blending together, their bodies crushed so tight that even air could not pass between them. Hina leaned back on the car and encouraged him to press her into it. He stepped closer and crushed her soft, warm body into the hard body of the car. He explored her mouth with his tongue and held her head in his hand.

Hina sucked his tongue into her mouth, parting her lips wide inviting him deeper while she pushed forward with her hips and ground her pussy on his cock in a way that told him that she would spread her legs right there if he just wanted to open his zip.

They broke the kiss slowly for want of breath and Hina squeezed herself against him even tighter, her cheek pressed to his cheeks.

"Sir, aap phir kab loge meri?" She spoke softly in his ear.

[When will you do me again?]

He gently pulled back before asking "Phir?"

She looked into his eyes and asked "I mean when will I see you again, Sir? I could come to your office, or…wherever you want."

Leaning in closer, he smiled in her eyes and said "I am not sure you noticed, honey, but your casting couch is done. You are going to be a model now."

Hina leaned back on his car and kept him close by keeping her arms around his neck "I know, Sir, but I...I want to see you again, on your couch, or desk, or whatever."

It was not lost on her that he had many beautiful girls around him. She had already met his secretary who was clearly his property. She was gorgeous and totally in love with him. Then he was married, probably to a supermodel. And Hina was sure that he could have any girl he wanted in his company. But she still wanted to meet him again. As the top boss, it was his right to have Hina as his whore and fuck her whenever he wanted. She really wanted him to exercise that right.

"You would like to meet again, even though you don't have to?" He said an eyebrow.

She nodded "Exactly, sir. I am not asking you to date me, but if you wanted to call me to your office, or your home, oh no, I remember you are married, but your office, like today?"

He leaned in and kissed her soft cheek gently "You are such a sweet girl, Hina."

At that, Hina's heart skipped a beat, it felt like he was about to dump her gently. Pulling back again a little, he looked in her eyes and said "My day is very meeting-heavy tomorrow, but what about the evening? Would you like to go out to dinner with me tomorrow night?"

"Would I?" Hina grinned "I would give my right arm to go on a date with you!"

Vikas grinned "You don't need to do that. You just need to say yes."

"Yes!" Hina said "Yes. Yes. Yes. A thousand times, yes."

He smiled and leaned in again. This time the kiss was even hotter and more passionate. Hina knew now that she would see him again the next day and it made her bolder and more confident in making out with him knowing that he had not rejected her. Her fingers that were massaging his neck moved up into hair and she pressed him into her while opening her lips wide so he could again push his tongue deep into her mouth. He licked the opening of her lips, teasing her before sliding his tongue into her mouth. Hina closed her lips around it and sucked it deeper into her mouth. Her breasts were so hard she could feel her nipples aching as they pressed into his chest. She could feel his dick getting hard between her legs. She instinctively pressed her pussy into his crotch and ground slowly, wantonly.

If he had opened his zip and entered her, Hina would have let him fuck her against his car. There was nothing she would deny him. She knew already from her one meeting with him that his cock was going to control her and she was not going to resist it. She was ready to surrender everything, he just had to reach out and take it. She was his wherever, whenever he wanted.

But instead of opening his zip, Vikas slowly pulled back, breaking the hot kiss that had become a very intense making out session by the side of the road. Hina pursued his lips with hers hoping to keep the kiss going but then she had to give up and reluctantly pull back.

"See you tomorrow?" He said looking into her eyes. He had stopped kissing her but they were still standing tightly pressed against each other. His tall, manly body was still dominating her, keeping her pinned against his car.

Hina nodded "Should I come to the office?"

"No," he shook his head "I will pick you up from here. Be ready about 8."

"Ok, thank you." Hina nodded, then she impulsively leaned in and kissed his cheek "I am looking forward to it." He had a slight stubble and Hina found that she loved rubbing her cheek on it.

"Me too." He kissed her neck lightly.

She pulled back and looked at him "Can you tell me what kind of place you will take me to, so I can dress right?"

He smiled and leaned in. "You are my gorgeous whore, Hina." Pressing his lips on her, he kissed her softly "You will look great everywhere you go. And you dress for me, not for the place. Who do you dress for?"

"I dress for my boss," Hina said. She wanted to say 'my owner' but didn't want to spoil things by overstepping in her eagerness "wherever he takes me is his choice."

"Good girl." He kissed her neck again.

"When you speak, it makes my pussy tingle." She whispered in his ear.

"That's good." He kissed her cheek "That means you will be my good whore."

"Yes, Sir." She squeezed herself against his chest "I will be your best whore."

"Should I go now?" Vikas asked, but as he started to step back Hina tightened her arms around him.

He looked at her and she shook her head.

"But if I don't go then I can't come back tomorrow, right?" He smiled.

She nodded.

"Then I need to go now." He said.

Again she shook her head. Then pulling him close to her, she pressed her lips on his. It led to another passionate kiss full of sexual charge. Hina was finding that the more she kissed him, the more she was hungry for him. She really wanted to take him inside and have him ravage her all night. She knew he had to go. She knew she would see him again tomorrow, but she could not bring herself to let him go.

Finally, Vikas walked her to her building entrance, and she went in with a final, quick kiss. She stood just inside the door and watched him get in the car. When he drove away she walked to the lift and pressed the button. She knew she was so wet that her thighs were soaked in her cunt juices.

[End of Book - Man of Power 3]

Thank you

Look, you might not think so, but I do really appreciate you buying my book. It tells me that my stories resonate with you and you enjoy them enough to buy them. I hope that you like them enough to recommend them to others as well. If you can take a minute to write a couple of lines in a review on the page where you bought this book, it would help others find my books which would help them and me both. And you will come off as a hero.

My Other books

Man of Power 1: Power Seduces All
Man of Power 2: Honeymoon Family Trip
Her Director's Property: Romeo Acquires New Talent
Oscar Bait: Romeo Starts a New Project
Tammy Starts a Business: When Beauty Meets Power

In the next book

- What is Shweta Tiwari's history with Vikas?
- Who is Riya Sen and why does she hate Vikas?
- What is Yami Gautam prepared to do to save her job?
- What happens to Hina's relationship once she becomes Vikas' property?
- Will Rashmika walk into Vikas' sphere of control once she joins us a temp clerk?
- Why is Sonal taking so much interest in Vikas?
- Will Parineeti ever get her wish to belong to Vikas?
- Pooja Hegde wants to join VisCom but will she agree to become Vikas' property?